A Voyage Through the Interstice

Michael Banister

Andrew Benzie Books
Martinez, California

Published by Andrew Benzie Books
www.andrewbenziebooks.com

Printed in the United States of America.

First Edition: February 2024

10 9 8 7 6 5 4 3 2 1

ISBN 978-1-950562-60-2

Cover and book design by Andrew Benzie

A dream of the world as it could have been…
and will become.

CHAPTER ONE

The Year 1497
July

Mattea Jacobella, wife of John Cabot, sat outside her favorite café at Bristol's seaport, enjoying the July sunshine and keeping an eye on her two younger sons, Lewis and Sancio, who were sailing their little toy sailboats in the narrow bay inlet. As she did almost every afternoon that summer, she nervously waited for a sighting of the caravel *Matthew* that her husband John and eldest son Sebastian had sailed out into the North Atlantic two months earlier.

John Cabot had repeatedly assured her of the little caravel's seaworthiness. John had a crew of 18 experienced seamen and enough food and water for a trip of up to six months. They carried little cargo; theirs was a voyage of exploration, not of trade. Although John Cabot fervently believed the continent of Asia lay across the Great Western Ocean, as did other English mariners, he needed proof in order to convince King Henry the Seventh to fund Cabot's proposal of a larger expedition of six ships and hundreds of sailors. Cabot believed the king was eager to explore the Atlantic now that the Spanish-funded fleet of Cristoforo Colombo had failed to return after five years at sea.

Mattea loved and admired her husband. He had years of experience as an experienced mariner. John Cabot had become a citizen of Venice 11 years before he married Mattea there in 1482. He told her many stories of his childhood in the Neapolitan town of Gaeta and in the city of Genoa. Mattea especially loved his stories of being a commercial mariner sailing to the shores of Arabia. When she asked him about the stories of him visiting the Muslim holy city of Mecca disguised as an Arab, he scoffed and denied it. "I would never have attempted such a foolish thing; non-Muslims who entered Mecca would be killed."

After John married Mattea, he adopted her son Sebastian as his own. Then John and Mattea had two more sons, Lewis and Sancio. A few years later, John got into financial trouble and had to leave Venice to avoid his creditors. They went to Spain.

He also had years of experience as a building contractor in Valencia and Sevilla. But he had had a run of bad luck in both cities and was finding it impossible to find work there in the building trades. He and Mattea also suspected the problem was the Spanish prejudice against Jews. Mattea had tried to keep her faith confidential, but people inevitably heard stories.

Because of the poor economy and the pervasive antisemitism in the Iberian Peninsula, Cabot revived his original idea of an exploratory ocean voyage. He convinced Mattea that the family should move to England to better his chances to find funding and approval for such a journey of exploration. The main reason for the move, he explained, was the failure of Admiral Cristoforo Colombo to return from his voyage. It had been five years since the departure of Colombo's little fleet of three ships. John Cabot, like many other mariners, believed that the fleet had encountered bad weather and was lost. If that was what had befallen Colombo, then the Spanish monarchs would be unlikely to risk funding another venture into the Atlantic.

King Henry, on the other hand, was receptive to Cabot's argument that an exploratory voyage further north would be a safer and shorter route to China. Many English mariners had sailed as far as Iceland, and the voyage that far was not considered overly dangerous. There were rumors of more islands, and perhaps another continent, further west. King Henry seemed ready to fund a small expedition once Cabot returned with good news from his exploratory voyage on the Matthew. Another reason for optimism on John and Mattea's part was that nobody in England knew she was Jewish.

Mattea's fear that her husband and eldest son would be lost at sea was something she tried to suppress. Mostly she did so by focusing on her enjoyment of the city of Bristol for its sophistication and climate, even though she missed her home and family in Venice.

"You look worried, my lady." The café owner himself looked worried, perhaps for the same reason. He sat down at her table, hoping that she would talk about what was worrying her.

"Yes, Robert, I suppose I shall always be worried. My husband is no reckless, inexperienced mariner, but one hears stories about the waters of the Atlantic Ocean."

Robert nodded, then smiled and said, "We all hear such stories, but more about the ocean farther south than the seas near Iceland. The Norse and others have fished the northern waters for many generations. And, it is supposed, Asia is much closer to England there than where the Spanish set sail from."

Mattea appreciated Robert's company and concern. She recalled their first meeting soon after her husband set sail across the Atlantic. She was aware that as Italians, she and John piqued the interest of many English people she met. And she was relieved that Robert and others didn't seem to harbor any prejudice toward Italians.

"Robert, I don't know how much you know about the situation in Spain. Our family was fortunate to be able to sail away from there without encountering any attacks from the Portuguese ships that seemingly patrol Spanish waters."

"You were indeed lucky, my lady. Those two countries have been at war since 1459, when Spanish ships attacked a Portuguese port. Soon thereafter, the Portuguese retaliated. Those attacks and counterattacks have continued since then. And everyone wonders whether the Spanish fleet under Colombo managed to escape being attacked by Portuguese vessels patrolling up and down the west coast of Europe. It has been five years since the fleet was reported to have left. The fleet is either doing business with China, or doing business with the fishes at the bottom of the Great Ocean."

Mattea nodded, but then added, "Still, I still do not understand the reason for such hostility between two Catholic countries. From what I've heard, though, perhaps the reason is that Spain has been jealous of Portugal's success in reaching Asia by rounding the tip of Africa. Another reason might be that Portugal blames Spain for blocking Portugal from expanding its slave trade in West Africa."

Robert began clearing Mattea's table and said, "Whatever the reason, King Henry has made a wise decision in considering your husband's request for funds for further exploration of the Atlantic Ocean."

"I suppose you are correct. But at the moment, I can't seem to put aside my worry about John's voyage, regardless of how short it is supposed to be." Mattea stood from her table and looked around for her sons. "Boys, come along. We must return home." Turning back to Robert, she said, "Thank you for keeping me company and making me feel somewhat more confident about my husband's voyage." She motioned for her boys to follow her, and together they left for home.

It wasn't a long walk from the water to the little stone cottage her family lived in. She enjoyed eavesdropping on her sons' conversation about how well their little boats fared in the water. The boys had made the boats themselves, with help from their older stepbrother Sebastian. He had designed the sails and made sure the strings were tied securely to the stern of each boat.

Even though Sebastian was a few years older—17 as opposed to 13 for Lewis and 11 for Sancio—he was not embarrassed when playing with them. He grew up with them even though he was their stepbrother. He had no memory of his early childhood. Sebastian's father, Marco Renaldi, had been killed during a maritime battle with the Ottoman Turks. A year later, Mattea Jacobella married John Cabot, whom Sebastian adored. Theirs was a happy family.

That evening, after Mattea had finished feeding the boys, it should have been bedtime for them. But the sun persisted in refusing to set until it was very late. Mattea kept the boys busy helping them with their school work, especially tutoring them in the English language. They were good students, especially in their language studies. They had learned several varieties of Spanish after having grown up in Spain. But even so, they, as well as Mattea, found English to be a remarkably puzzling language. Mattea and John had learned Arabic when they lived in Spain, but the boys found no interest in that language, let alone proficiency.

Finally, when Mattea and the boys could no longer stay alert that evening, they went to bed. The distant sounds of water and wind and seabirds made it easy to fall asleep.

*   *   *

Her dream was without a doubt the strangest she'd ever had. She was on a ship. In fact, the dream told her the ship had something to do with her husband, although John was not part of the crew. The members of the crew were busy sailing the ship and paid no attention to her. They were speaking a strange language that she had never heard before. They had coffee-colored skin with straight black hair and brown eyes. A few of them appeared to be African, with black skin and curly hair. Perhaps the strangest thing of all was that many of them were women; the captain shouting orders was a woman. And that woman actually glanced at Mattea and smiled. The woman's smile woke Mattea up.

The dream troubled Mattea so much that she could no longer sleep. She got up, checked on the boys, and went into the kitchen. She sat down and looked out the window. It was almost dawn. She got up and started the kettle for tea. Sitting back, she tried to recall as many details of the dream as she could. It seemed important, very important, to do that. She got up again to pour the boiling water into the teapot, then rummaged through the kitchen desk looking for paper and something to write with. She sat back down and began writing down as much of the dream as she could.

One aspect that impacted her most in the dream was the presence of female crew members on the ship. Not just the crew, but the captain herself. And the fact that the captain looked at her and even smiled at her. And what about the Africans? Now that she remembered the Africans, she recalled that some were actually speaking Arabic, not the language of the other crew members. Arabic? Why? Were the ship and the dream from Africa?

Her sons must have heard her moving about in the kitchen because, as she poured her tea, they came into the kitchen looking puzzled to see their mother up before dawn. Mattea put away her paper and got up from the table to make breakfast.

August

Mattea left the boys with their tutor and walked out of the house, intending to do some shopping in town before heading over to the seaport. But she didn't get far before she saw Robert's servant running toward her. "Ma'am, we have seen your husband's ship coming into the harbor! It will be docked soon."

She followed the servant to the harbor, trying to slow her racing heart. When they arrived, she could see dock workers securing the Matthew to the pier. Mattea walked quickly up the gangplank as soon as it had been lowered and secured. Not seeing John on the top deck, she walked down to the captain's cabin. John had his back to her and was talking to one of the sailors. She ran up to her husband and hugged him from behind. John turned and kissed her. "My love, I have so much to tell you. The voyage... it was a success, but not what I expected. Let me finish this paperwork while you walk around on the ship. Sebastian is below dealing with the cargo."

Mattea descended two levels to the lower hold where she saw her son talking to crewmen. He saw her, walked over and said, "Mother! The voyage... I don't know what to say! Have you talked to father?"

"Yes. He is busy with paperwork but will join me on the dock. Are you free? Shall we leave the ship?"

He took leave of the crewmen and turned back to Mattea. Together they walked up to the top deck and descended the gangplank to the dock. Mattea said, "Let's have a seat on a bench beneath the trees out of the sun."

Mattea was expecting Sebastian to begin telling her details of the voyage, but he said he wanted to wait until his father emerged from the ship. After a few minutes, they could see John leave the ship carrying a long, painted and carved stick. When he reached them, he handed Mattea the stick and said, "My men found this on the beach where we first landed. It was near the remains of a campfire. We saw animal droppings. It was all forested. We thought we saw a few people run into the forest. We followed a trail into the forest for a bit before turning back to the ship. The trees were like ours here in England."

Mattea held the stick and turned it from end to end. "There are holes in it, one hole in each end. What do you suppose the stick was used for?"

"A tool of some sort, but we don't know."

Mattea said, "Was that only land you saw? You were gone for almost two months."

"We saw other land from our ship, but only put into shore one time. The land was to the north of the strait we were sailing through.

We couldn't tell whether the land was an island or part of a mainland. The crew was anxious to return home, and our food was beginning to run out. But I'm planning another voyage, this time with at least four ships and perhaps 100 men."

Mattea pursed her lips and said, "100 men and one woman—your wife! I'm going with you. And so are all three boys, not just Sebastian."

"I'm not sure King Henry will agree, but I will ask him."

"No, don't ask–tell! We will board your ship when the time comes, at dawn. All you need to do before then is prepare the captain's cabin for us."

Mattea loved the way the rugged sea captain, John Cabot, her husband, laughed. She smiled and said, "John, I'm serious. We're going with you. You just do what I said and everything will be fine." This time, Cabot just smiled. Sebastian also smiled, but with a tinge of nervousness. Cabot took Mattea's hand and together they stood. Cabot looked at Sebastian and said, "Son, I would like you to go back aboard and finish giving the unloading instructions to the crew. Your mother and I will meet you back at the house."

CHAPTER TWO

November 1497

Mattea was surprised when she answered the knock at the door of their cottage. A soldier and a boy who looked to be no more than 11 or 12 stood there, a shy boy who nonetheless strived to hide his shyness and instead project an air of calm authority. "My Lady, I am told that Captain Cabot resides here. You are his wife?"

"Yes, my husband lives here with me and our family. Shall I send one of our sons to go fetch him? Who shall I say seeks to speak to him?"

"My Lady, it is my father, King Henry, who commands your husband's presence at the Royal Maritime House here in the city. If you can, please have your son inform the captain of this summons."

"You are Prince Arthur, then?"

"Yes, Madam. Very pleased to meet you. I am hopeful we will be able to speak more when you arrive at the Residence." With that, Prince Arthur bowed, turned, and he and the soldier left.

Mattea closed the door and called for Sebastian. "Son, go out in the garden and call your brothers to the house. Then I would like you to go to the market, find your father, and ask him to return home. The King requests our presence in the city."

"The King? Are you joking?"

"I am serious. Go, do as I say."

It took Sebastian quite some time to find his father in the crowded, busy market. It was the time of the harvest and most farmers had wheeled and carted their produce and livestock into the city in hopes of good prices and not too much competition. After more than an hour of searching, Sebastian found his father bargaining with a farmer over the price of a sheep. "Father, mother asks that you return home at once."

"At once? Why? I have more purchases to make, and the prices are very good. Tell me why she wants me to return home now."

Sebastian looked around, and motioned for his father to step away from the pen holding the sheep. "Father, Prince Arthur came to the house and told mother that the King commanded you to come to his residence in the city. He wouldn't give the reason."

Cabot smiled and said, "Ah, I think I know. His Majesty wishes to learn more about our voyage and discuss the next voyage." He turned back to the owner of the sheep and said, "I'll accept your price. Tie the sheep to this rope and I'll take her with me."

Cabot, Sebastian and the sheep walked along the road as Cabot pumped his son for more information, but none was forthcoming. "He wouldn't say more than that the king commands your presence at the residence. But father, we were surprised at how young the prince is. He's much younger than I!"

"Yes, I know about Arthur. He's young, but nonetheless the oldest son and the heir. He'll be king someday. By all accounts, he'll make a good king."

*   *   *

Cabot had only met with the king twice in the past, both times in the early spring when Cabot proposed his idea of a voyage across the Great Ocean to Asia. But those meetings had taken place in London, and Cabot had not brought his wife or Sebastian to the meeting. On this occasion, Mattea insisted on attending the meeting with Sebastian.

She needn't have worried about upsetting the king by accompanying her husband. The king seemed pleased to meet her and greeted her warmly. "I have set out food and refreshments in the dining room, so why don't we eat and drink before we begin our discussion?"

Mattea smiled and nodded. John said, "That would be wonderful, Your Majesty. We left the house as soon as we could and have not had our evening meal."

After the king ordered a servant to set the table with additional place settings, everyone stood and entered the dining room. They took their seats and dinner was served.

As they began eating, Cabot congratulated the king on his recent victory over the pretender to the throne, Perkin Warbeck. The king smiled, "Thank you. That troublesome man will trouble me no longer. I ordered him hanged after he confessed his crimes against me."

Then the king brought up the reason for his summons. "Captain Cabot, I am sure you have heard rumors of what probably happened to Admiral Colombo's expedition to Asia. Most likely, his fleet has been lost, otherwise he would have returned to Spain by now. Since that seems to be the case, I am even more resolved to proceed with your proposal for an additional expedition. However, I don't think it would be wise to devote five ships and hundreds of men to the expedition. I still have concerns about the French, despite the current period of calm between us. I am prepared to order two ships, fully loaded with supplies and with full crews selected by you. One ship is a carrack named Le Michel and the other is a caravel named La

Cristianne. Our naval forces captured them from Perkin Warbeck's navy. Would that be satisfactory?"

Cabot paused before answering. Then with a smile he said, "Yes, Your Majesty, that would be more than satisfactory. As for the French, I doubt they will pose any further difficulty against England. Nevertheless, your decision to be wary of the French is wise. And you are no doubt aware of the state of war between Spain and Portugal. Repeated attacks on one another's ports have brought their maritime ambitions to a virtual standstill. Observers cannot understand the reason for this state of war. My proposal to sail to Asia across the Atlantic can succeed with a fleet of two ships as well as with four."

The king nodded. "Good. Now… I have one other subject I feel I must bring up." Turning to Mattea, he paused with an embarrassed look on his face and said, "Madame Jacobella. It has come to my attention that the reason you and your family departed Spain might not have been because of the economy or the war with Portugal. Before I tell you what I've heard, perhaps you would care to elaborate?"

Mattea was stunned. She, her husband and her children had been very careful not to mention her religion. She and John had always believed that because they were citizens of Venice, they wouldn't have to face suspicion as to her being Jewish. But that belief was put to the test in Spain, where anti-Jewish rancor was widespread. Perhaps one of their Spanish "friends," or one of Sebastian's playmates, spread the rumor that she was Jewish. Now that rumor had apparently followed them north to England.

"Yes, Your Majesty is correct that our departure from the Iberian Peninsula was not only due to the lack of work. The more pressing reason was the fact that I am Jewish." She paused, and then continued. "Surely, my religion will not prevent my husband from securing your support for the voyage across the Great Ocean. He is a devout Catholic, and we have raised our boys in that Faith."

King Henry sighed. "My lady, I must apologize for the prejudices of my people, but most especially the prejudices of our Church. At the Church's insistence, a law that Jews may not live in England was promulgated over 200 years ago, largely due to the blind ignorance of priests." The king took another breath before continuing. "I personally harbor no prejudice or ill will toward Jews. But on the other hand, I am not at liberty to overturn such an entrenched law. The Church would waste no time fomenting plots against me and my government. I cannot risk further instability so soon after the troublesome Perkin Warbeck affair."

Mattea nodded and said, "I quite understand the situation." Then she turned to her husband, smiled, and turned back to the king. "My husband and I had discussed his upcoming plans for another ocean voyage, and decided that I and our boys would accompany him on that voyage. Should that meet your approval, then the question of a Jew living in England would become moot."

John Cabot managed to suppress his reaction, but King Henry smiled. "Surely, that is the best idea I have heard, one that I hadn't considered. I had feared the alternative should the rumors gain further credence, especially among the clergy." He paused, took a sip of his wine, and continued. "Captain Cabot, Mrs. Jacobella, I will order the captain's cabin on the larger of the two ships to be modified and enlarged to accommodate your family. I understand your son Sebastian is already an accomplished sailor, so he can sleep with the crew as one of the Mates. The two younger boys, Lewis and Sancio, are 13 and 11 if memory serves. They can work as crewmen if you wish. Or they can simply be passengers. I would imagine they will prefer to work with the crew." The king turned to John. "Captain Cabot, I will leave the arrangements in your worthy hands. I believe the weather will not be accommodating until the end of winter. Perhaps set a date for the end of April?"

"Your Majesty, I am humbled and grateful for your kindness and generosity. I will do as you suggest."

At that, everyone stood. The king said, "I have other business to conduct at this time. Please do keep me informed as to your progress concerning this voyage."

CHAPTER THREE

The Year 1498
June

It was a warm, sunny morning at the seaport. The two ships and their crews were ready—Le Michel, the large carrack and La Cristianne, the smaller caravel. Crew members had been hired a month earlier—15 men plus Sebastian on La Cristianne, 18 men plus Captain Cabot, Madame Jacobella and their two younger sons on Le Michel. The Captain's Cabin on the carrack had been expanded to sleep John and Mattea; their sons would work and sleep with the crew. John chose one of the Norsemen, Arne, to be Captain on the caravel La Cristianne. Sebastian was proud to have been chosen as Arne's First Mate due to his experience sailing on the earlier voyage across the northern ocean.

John chose an Irishman, Shay Black, as his First Mate on Le Michel. Mattea became the Ship's Doctor on Le Michel, which included not only treating injuries but compounding medicines, a skill Mattea had mastered at university in Venice. John was well respected as Captain due to his experience on the earlier voyage across the Atlantic.

Mattea and John were pleased at the makeup of the crew. Because of stories of the experiences of the Norsemen who had explored the lands to the west, Cabot had decided to recruit men from Scandinavia as well as from England. He and Mattea had become conversant in the Norse language during their time in England. They decided to hire a tutor for their boys.

*   *   *

Cabot had explained to Mattea and their sons earlier that their route across the northern sea would bring them past Greenland and Iceland before continuing on as far as Cabot's earlier expedition had reached. "My goal is to reach the shores of China, beyond those two islands."

Now Cabot was about to address the crew members before everyone would board the ships and prepare for departure. "Men, a few of you were with me on my earlier voyage. This time, we will follow that same route, but instead of making landfall at the same location, we will proceed further west and turn north. I do not know whether that land mass is an island or peninsula, but we will sail north until we determine the nature of the land. My plan is to find a safe harbor, spend at least a month there, and explore the land. I also hope to make contact with the people who live there." When he said this, several of the men became more alert.

"Those of you who were on the previous voyage might remember seeing people running into the forest as we explored what appeared to be a campsite. I am told that Swedes and Norse had settled on one large island near our destination. Perhaps any people we encounter will be familiar with that language."

At this point, Captain Arne of the caravel La Cristianne spoke up. "Captain Cabot, what you say has reminded me of stories about Norsemen sailing to the lands beyond Greenland and establishing settlements on those lands. Even though some of the settlements were ultimately abandoned hundreds of years later, and many people returned to their homeland, some stories they brought back with them spoke of encounters with local people that were sometimes violent encounters. Some Norsemen called those people 'Skraeling,' accusing them of stealing items from camps. Some settlers told stories describing the Skraeling as uninterested in learning from the Norse. However, other accounts speak of Skraelings more favorably, learning to trade with the settlers, even learning some of the Norse language. So, Captain, we don't know what kind of folk we shall encounter as we venture beyond our landing site."

*   *   *

The two ships set out at dawn the next day. Cabot had decided to make for the same land he had reached in his previous voyage. Their voyage took slightly more than two months and was largely uneventful, except for the sight of many whales—Grays, Bowheads, Fin Whales, Blue Whales and Belugas. Cabot ordered the men not to disturb the whales, instead instructing them to cast nets for the plentiful cod in the schools they passed.

October 1498

When the ships came within view of a location near the one Cabot had visited on the earlier voyage, he ordered them to proceed further west and turn north as soon as they determined they were truly on the west side of the land instead of inside a bay.

After several hours, they passed through what appeared to be a strait between the land mass to their right and an even larger landmass to the south. At that point, Cabot signaled for the ships to turn and proceed north along the coast. Before long, he saw that they were about to enter a bay of some sort. Cabot ordered the two ships to proceed further into the bay and drop lead-weighted lead lines into the water to determine the depth, which would determine whether they could drop anchor. He turned to Mattea and said, "I believe the crews deserve a rest. We should spend the night on shore. The beach to our left looks fairly free of forest and the shoreline doesn't appear to be too rocky."

*   *   *

It was already dusk by the time both crews had disembarked. They hurriedly cleared an area some distance from the shore and set out tarps and blankets. Dry wood was gathered and a cooking area was set up. Several of the sailors managed to catch several large fish. Others walked into the forest and gathered what they hoped were edible plants and fruits. Sebastian said to Arne, "Well, it doesn't appear that we will starve, at least not tonight."

Arne replied, "I will set a watch around our little camp to make sure we aren't threatened by animals or people."

By midnight, the exhausted crews had succumbed to exhaustion and full stomachs. Sebastian, Cabot, Shay and Arne were the only sailors wakeful enough to stand guard. Other than seeing furtive movements in the nearby forest, they passed the night in peace, finally falling asleep just before dawn.

*   *   *

After a breakfast of hard ship's biscuit and tea, the crews got underway. They exited the bay and turned due north, following the coastline. For the most part, the coast was a long sandy beach backed up by dense forest. There were several inlets and small bays, and the ships took advantage of the opportunity to explore them, fish and take on fresh water from the streams flowing into the bays. By the end of the first day, Cabot ordered the crews to drop anchor and go ashore to get some rest on solid ground.

CHAPTER FOUR

First Encounter

By midafternoon on the next day, Captain Cabot took the lead ship into a narrow strait. It didn't take long to pass through the strait, which veered slightly northeast.

As the ships were exiting the strait, Cabot saw a sheltered, circular bay on their south. To his astonishment, he saw a group of a dozen or more primitive dwellings set back from the beach at the edge of a forested area. He signaled to the caravel ahead to drop anchor at the mouth of the bay and determine the depth. After an hour, Captain Arne signaled back that the bay was deep enough for both ships to enter.

Cabot signaled to Arne's caravel to proceed slowly into the bay and then drop anchor to await the larger carrack. Cabot ordered two ships' boats lowered into the bay, and he, his first mate, and two oarsmen got into the boats. Arne had done the same from the caravel. The two ships' boats were now less than 100 yards from the dwellings. The two captains ordered their crews to row slowly to the beach and be on the alert for any sign of trouble.

The boats reached the shore together and the crews hopped out when the water was shallow enough. As they pulled the boats up onto the shore, they spotted a group of half a dozen men standing in front of one of the huts watching them.

Arne said to Cabot, "Captain, let me approach them first. One of the men has the appearance of a Norseman; the others appear to be natives." Cabot nodded and ordered the rest of the men to stand ready to join Arne on his signal.

Arne walked slowly up the beach. When he was close enough to the group of men in front of the hut, he stopped, raised his hands and said in Norse, "We come from your land across the Great Ocean. We come in peace. We only wish to learn more about this land. Will you allow us to approach?"

The Norse-looking man looked astonished. Rubbing his beard, he looked from side to side at his companions and said something to them in a language Arne did not understand. Turning back to Arne, the man smiled and said, "Well, it has been many a year since I've heard my native tongue from anyone but my few countrymen still living on this island. I was barely an adult when most of the Norse left this island. Some twenty of us Norsemen chose to remain here, married and had children. We live in small communities along the top of this island and another community near the bottom of the island." He motioned to the ships in the harbor and said, "Your ships are unlike any we've ever seen. Where are they from?"

Arne began to translate the conversation for Cabot and the others, but Cabot stopped him. "Arne, I understood him well enough. Let me put my Norse language to work. I will explain who we are and why we have come here."

He turned to the Norseman. "I am John Cabot, commander of these two ships and captain of the larger one." Pointing to Arne, he said, "This is Captain Arne, who is captain of the smaller of the two ships at anchor. He is Norse also, as are many of our crew members. I am not Norse myself, but I learned some of the language on a previous voyage. We have 34 crew members, including my wife and family. Will you allow us to come ashore?"

The Norseman smiled and said, "My name is Erik. Yes, of course. Have your men and family come ashore. I will send for others to join us. Most of them are hunting and gathering wood for the evening's meal. I will have them prepare a feast. I am sure you will be glad to join us!"

*   *   *

Mattea and her two younger sons were the first to disembark from Le Michel. As the rest of Le Michel's crew disembarked, Sebastian supervised the crew members disembarking from La Cristianne. Many of the crew took advantage of the chance to swim to the shore from the ships. Mattea told Lewis and Sancio to do the same in order to exercise their stiff bodies. Mattea herself directed the offloading of one of her trunks containing clothes. Once that was accomplished, she waded back into the water and swam back and forth between the boats and the shore.

After an hour, all of the crew were on shore and the ships well anchored. Arne and Erik were deep in conversation when Captain Cabot approached. "Captain, Erik tells me that his wife is native to this land but she and the children are conversant in the Norse language. Erik has told me that there are perhaps several dozen Norse people living here. Communication between our crews and the people of this community should not be difficult."

Cabot nodded and said to Erik, "Would it be agreeable to arrange a meeting of some sort to allow us to learn from one another?"

Erik nodded. Just then, someone shouted. Erik, Cabot and Arne turned and saw a group of men and women emerging from the forest carrying long tree branches on which were spitted deer and what looked like pigs.

Erik turned back and said to Cabot, "I suggest we sit down together at tonight's feast and talk."

Cabot nodded and turned to the crews assembled on the shore.

"Men, we're going to join these people tonight for a meal. In the meantime, several of you with experience as cooks and kitchen workers should volunteer to help with the meal preparations." As Mattea walked up, Cabot said to Erik, "This is my wife, Mattea Jacobella. She is our ships' doctor. Two of our younger sons are still enjoying the pleasant water, and our older son is helping the crews secure the ships."

Erik extended his hand to Mattea and said, "I am very pleased to meet you, but I am a bit surprised to hear that a woman and children are part of the crew."

"Yes, it is unusual for a woman and children to join an expedition such as this, but our king thought it a wonderful idea. If any of your people have any illnesses, I might be able to help."

Erik said, "Let us walk to our community house at the edge of the wood and get comfortable." Cabot, Mattea and Arne followed Erik to the building as they continued their conversation.

The building was a simple structure, some 30 feet long by 15 feet wide, built simply of young trees lashed together with strips of leather. The roof reminded Arne of simple thatch roofs common in the English and Irish countryside. Arne pointed to several other structures and asked why they appeared to be damaged. Erik replied, "Our community has been plagued by attacks from people from the land across this channel, the Mikmak people. They are numerous. Perhaps they feel they need our land to expand into. I don't know their motivation. There haven't been many attacks so far, but we worry that they will increase and become more destructive. So far, no one has been killed or injured."

Arne asked, "Are these Mikmak people Skraeling?"

Erik flinched and replied, "We do not like the term Skraeling, which is a pejorative term invented by the Norse when they first arrived. The Mikmaks call themselves Mikmak. They are not related to our people on this island, who are the Beothuk people."

Mattea had been following the conversation as she observed the handful of simple structures at the edge of the forest. "Erik, do you think your people would be offended if some of our crew helped them construct more defensible villages?"

Cabot turned to Mattea, "That's an intriguing idea."

Mattea continued, "Among our crew are many former carpenters and masons who joined us out of a sense of opportunity to explore new lands. They, and indeed all the rest of us, would welcome the opportunity to spend some time in your beautiful country."

Erik looked astonished. "Your offer is most welcome. I must confess that our dwellings are primitive. When our ancestors arrived here decades ago, their purpose was exploration, not colonization. And the local people, the Beothuks, lived in simple circular structures of skin-covered tree trunks and branches. Our Norse ancestors who remained strove to improve the living conditions, but as you can see our homes are primitive. Any help you can provide would be most welcome!"

For the next few hours, most of the crews unloaded what they thought they would need for an extended stay. Cabot engaged with several community members in a discussion of possible areas where a sleeping structure could be built for the crew members.

During a pause in that discussion, Cabot commented, "I think the first thing we could do is erect a defensive fence around your community. We could use small or mid-sized tree trunks aligned vertically, with as little free space in between as possible. The trunks would be sharpened or pointed at the top, and would be driven into the ground and perhaps reinforced with additional construction. The height of the fence should probably be twice as high as a Norseman. That type of fence would be susceptible to fire, so it would be a good idea to build permanent structures of stone between the wooden fence and the shore." Sebastian, Shay and the two younger Cabot boys volunteered to form a group to explore the forest in search of suitable trees to cut for possible use as building material.

At that point, three community members emerged from a large

structure that looked like a kitchen and gestured to Erik. Erik turned to Cabot and asked if several of his crew would care to assist in preparing the evening meal. Mattea and the ships' cooks volunteered and followed Erik to the kitchen.

While the kitchen was busy with cooking, other community members arrived from their dwellings further inland and introduced themselves to the sailors.

A busy two months: November, December 1498

During the next two days the crew members and local people began cutting slim 10-foot-tall trees and dragging them to a clearing some distance from the shore. John and Mattea directed the placement of the trees in a long arc in front of where the island's people had built their structures.

The following two weeks were occupied with digging three-foot-deep holes along the perimeter of the clearing. As some men and women dug the holes, others trimmed branches from each tree and sharpened the top end of the tree. Still others gathered stones that would be used to fill the holes around the buried tree shafts. Cabot asked several masons to make adobe by mixing grass with the abundant clay soil. By the end, more than 40 holes had been dug, an equal number of trees were trimmed of branches, and piles of small stones were placed near each hole.

At the beginning of the third week, the actual erection of the protective wall began. As pairs of crewmen placed a trimmed pole into each hole, local people poured a wet mixture of adobe, straw and small pebbles into the hole around the pole. Once the hole was filled to overflowing, the stone-adobe mixture was firmly tamped down to ensure the pole remained firmly rooted and upright. By the end of the fourth day, a defensive perimeter of 40 closely spaced sharpened trees guarded the Beothuk village from invaders.

The next task took two weeks. The ship's masons directed a small army of villagers to create a head-high stone wall held together with adobe. The wall ran the entire length of the defensive perimeter of sharpened trees and continued beyond the trees to the edge of the forest where most of the villagers' dwellings were. The front section of the adobe structure stood eight to nine paces outside the tree perimeter, and was three feet wide with a flat top on which a person could stand. On the inside of the adobe wall, the workers had installed steps every few feet to allow access to the top of the wall. Once the wall was finished, a supply of stones and arrows was placed along the top.

As the villagers and crewmen worked on the two perimeter walls, other crewmen with construction skills were erecting buildings for housing and community activities.

CHAPTER FIVE

Looking for China

After two more weeks, the community and the sailors had settled into a more relaxed routine. Erik and several other villagers, both Norse and Beothuk, were telling Cabot, Mattea, and Arne about the history and geography of the area. When Cabot asked about the land of China, he was met with puzzled expressions. Cabot said, "We were told stories of a vast continent called China. A European explorer named Marco Polo traveled there from Europe some 200 years ago. He went east overland and reached China. He spent years as a guest of the emperor, returned to Europe and wrote an account of his journey."

Erik replied, "Well, your ships have traveled west, not east. We Norse have made only a few explorations of the lands to the west of this island. But we have heard nothing of a land called China. Perhaps if you continue your voyage in the westward direction, you will find China. But you will not be able to sail your ships any further west from here. The land on the other side of the strait blocks your way. There are many hostile Mikmak people in that land."

Mattea turned to her husband and said, "Perhaps if we voyage south the way we came, we will find a passage west."

At that point, a Beothuk man commented. "My name is Gobidin, which means 'eagle' in the Norse language. My people have several communities inland from the coast you followed in coming up here. My sister Abidish and I have visited those communities and have heard stories about a vast continent to the west of there, across the open ocean. Perhaps several of us Beothuk could accompany you and introduce you to our people south of here. They may have more information about that land. They may not speak the Norse language, but the Beothuks who accompany you could act as interpreters."

January 1499

The expedition was almost ready to depart. The captain and crew were finishing up their explanations of how the two ships would operate during the voyage. Gwinya, one of the female Beothuks who had been selected to join the crew, said, "Captain Cabot, are the ships ready for the return voyage south? It would be good that we leave soon, as the weather looks threatening." Gwinya's expression was serious. She pointed to the small island visible not far to the north and said, "The sea between here and that island is already becoming ice bound. Since we will sail south, perhaps we will avoid an encounter with ice."

"Yes, I was aware of the ice. And yes, we are almost ready to depart." Turning to face the crews and community members gathered there he said, "Six Beothuk people will join us on the voyage, which should not take more than three days' sailing. We have chosen three women: Gwinya, Abidish and Cosweet; and three men: Gobidin, Kooreh, and Matuis. All are conversant in Norse and have expressed a desire to introduce us and our mission to their brethren on the southern coast."

The two ships and their expanded crews departed at first light the next morning. Cabot was right. There was no ice, and the weather became significantly warmer as they sailed south. In the afternoon of the third day, the ships reached the same small bay where they had stopped earlier. Cabot could see the remains of several structures and boats. They looked like they had been burned.

Gobidin informed Cabot that they should enter the bay and plan to remain for perhaps two or three days to allow Gobidin and Abidish to search for Beothuk people living in the nearby forest. Cabot agreed and ordered the crews and passengers to go ashore and prepare a camp.

The first morning on land, Gobidin and Abidish ventured along a well-worn trail into the forest in the hope of contacting some of their brethren living in that portion of the island. After an hour, Abidish motioned to her brother to be still and silent. Then she said, "Do you hear them? The cooing. Like doves. Don't you recall? That used to be their signal to whoever was coming along the path to stop and wait. One who does so would thereby show themselves to be a friend."

Gobidin nodded and the two of them stood stock still. After a few minutes, two figures emerged from the trees on the left. The younger person was a young woman, perhaps twenty years old, very tall, reddish-brown skin, and long black hair. Her eyes were jet black, although that could have been from astonishment at seeing Gobidin and Abidish.

The other person looked like a positively ancient man. But he stood straight with his arms crossed in front of him. He was not as tall as the young woman, nor was his hair as long. It was black with streaks of gray and white throughout.

Both wore leggings and long coats made of leather. Their feet were shod in leather and tied around their ankles with thongs.

The old man spoke first. "Welcome, brother and sister of the north. I am Dogajavik; this is my stepdaughter, Aponi. What brings you to our country? Are the Mikmak people still continuing with their attacks to the north? As you probably noticed, they have attacked our community here on the bay."

Gobidin walked forward, extended his arms and embraced Dogajavik. Abidish took a few steps toward Aponi and smiled.

Gobidin said, "I am Gobidin. Yes, the Mikmak continue to plague us also. But that is not why we are here. We have come as crew members on two large ships. The captains and their sailors are from across the Great Ocean to the east, from the land of the Norsemen. They seek a country they call China."

Aponi turned to Abidish and asked, "Who are you?"

"I am Abidish, Gobidin's sister. We have come inland from our ships seeking our Beothuk brethren to the south of our land." She paused, looked more closely at Aponi, and said, "But now that I see you up close, I am not sure you are Beothuk."

Aponi looked at her and said, "You are right. My people are from a distant land across the western sea. They are the Onondaga people. I was but a girl on one of their boats that a group of Mikmak people sank as we were exploring the strait to the southwest of this island. I alone was rescued, saved by Beothuk people and adopted by Dogajavik."

Dogajavik smiled at Aponi and said, "There will be time later to discuss family history." Turning to Abidish he said, "Perhaps you should lead us to your ships. I think your people will want to hear what we have to say."

The walk back to the bay did not take long. When they arrived, Aponi and Dogajavik were astonished at the sight of the huge sailing ships. The sailors and Beothuk passengers were engaged in constructing a rudimentary shelter some distance inland from the bay, and now stood staring at the four who had emerged from the forest.

Cabot walked up and introduced himself in Norse. "I am John Cabot, captain of these ships. I and my crew are from England, across the Great Ocean. We are on a voyage seeking to make contact with a land called China, which we believe is to the west of this island. We have just sailed south from a Beothuk community at the tip of this island."

Before Abidish could translate for Dogajavik and Aponi,

Dogajavik said, "No need. Many of us in the Beothuk communities are familiar with the Norse language. The Norse lived on this island for many years before most of them left. Several remained and married into different communities." He walked forward and extended his hand to Cabot. "I am Dogajavik and this young woman with me is Aponi. Perhaps we can join your camp and discuss your plans."

Cabot smiled and replied, "Actually, myself and the crew would like to meet members of your community. Abidish and Gobidin have told us of their earlier visits to your community here. Would it be possible for myself, our ships' officers, and our Beothuk passengers to visit your community?"

Dogajavik said, "I think it would be better if the people in our small nearby community came here to meet you. I am sure we would like to learn more about your voyage and your mission. And especially these ships! I have never seen anything like that."

As they were talking, Mattea walked up with Sebastian and said, "I overheard your conversation and I agree with both suggestions. But first, let's invite Dogajavik's people here for a discussion of our mission, and a tour of our ships. We will prepare a meal. Several of our crewmen went hunting and brought back animals that one of our Beothuk passengers calls 'galipu.' After that feast, we would love to visit your community."

Dogajavik smiled. "I see that you have constructed a fire pit and cleared an area for eating and sleeping. Very good. I will accept your offer." Turning to Aponi he said, "Perhaps you should return to our village and invite our people to a feast!"

Sebastian stepped forward and said, "If you don't mind, Aponi, I would like to accompany you. I would love to see your village."

Aponi smiled and said, "It would be my pleasure to show you my home and introduce you to my people." She turned and began walking toward the forest. Sebastian walked alongside her.

"Tell me about yourself and your people," Aponi said as they walked.

"Actually, the people on these two ships are from different lands. Perhaps 40 or so are from the continent of Europe, a vast land to the east across the Great Ocean. Most of those are Norse people from Scandinavia. Five of the rest – my parents, two brothers and myself—are from an area of Europe called Italy. Other European crewmembers come from England, Ireland and Scotland. Six Beothuk people are our guests from the northern tip of this island. Our captain, my stepfather, John Cabot, thought it would be wise to invite some Beothuk people to join our voyage to assist us in communicating with the people of this land."

"Did you say Captain Cabot is your stepfather? What happened to your real father?"

"Yes, Cabot is my stepfather. He married my mother, Mattea Jacobella, after her husband, Marco Renaldi, my actual father, was killed by Turkish pirates in a sea battle when I was a baby. I don't remember him." Sebastian paused and looked around as they entered the forest. Then he said to Aponi. "Please tell me about yourself. You look different from the other Beothuk people here and in the north."

"That's because I am not Beothuk. My people are the Onondaga people, from a land to the west of this island. I was a ten-year-old child on one of their boats exploring these islands when the boat sank after striking some offshore rocks in an attempt to escape an attack by a Mikmak ship. I alone survived. I managed to swim to the rocky shore of an island. Eventually, a passing boat saw me and rescued me. I was adopted by a Beothuk family, Dogajavik's family."

"Oh, the Onondaga lands are to the west? Are they close to China? That is the country we are seeking."

"I have not heard of China. But as I said, I was very young when I was separated from other Onondaga people on that boat."

"Do the Beothuk know anything of the lands to the west of here?"

"Perhaps some of the elders do. When we gather tonight there will be questions and answers." At that point, they saw they were leaving the forest and entering a clearing. "Ah, here is my village. I will take you to our headman's house and introduce you. Then you will meet others."

CHAPTER SIX

"The big waterway"

The village consisted of not more than a dozen homes arrayed in a large circle around one large building that looked to be some sort of meeting hall. The homes were constructed of young trees lashed together, covered with thick thatch of some kind. There were large gaps between the trees forming the front of each home, leaving a doorway from the ground to the roof. There were window holes cut on the sides of the structures. Tall trees formed the sides of the meeting hall. Each end of the hall was open, and several windows had been cut on each side.

Aponi led Sebastian to the entrance of the meeting hall, where a small group of people had gathered inside. Aponi said, "I will enter first and speak to Mondicuet, the headman of our village. You should wait here until Mondicuet acknowledges you. I will speak to him in Norse, a language that he and several of our community know."

Sebastian watched Aponi enter and approach the people sitting at the head of a long table. He couldn't tell what they were doing; it looked like a meeting rather than a dinner. Moments after Aponi began speaking to Mondicuet, he arose, looked at Sebastian and smiled. Then he motioned for him to enter and come to the table.

Sebastian walked to within a few feet of the table, where Aponi

35

introduced him to the group, "Friends, our community has been blessed with visitors from across the Great Ocean. They are in two huge sailing ships that just this morning dropped anchor. This young man is Sebastian Cabot, one of the captains. He has come to invite us to meet the crews and passengers. Six of the passengers are our esteemed cousins from the north of this island."

The others at the table stood. Mondicuet greeted Sebastian, "Welcome to our village. You come just as our little group here was discussing some business. Come and sit for a while and tell us about yourself. I will send someone to let the other villagers know of your arrival."

Sebastian smiled, bowed, and walked to the table and waited for Mondicuet to be seated. Then he said, "The king of my country sends greetings and offers of friendship. His name is Henry, the seventh king with that name in our history. He has tasked our expedition with seeking trade with the peoples of China."

Mondicuet motioned for Sebastian and Aponi to be seated. Sebastian said, "My father, John Cabot, is the lead captain of our expedition. He sends his greetings and invites the people of this village to join us at our camp on the coast and have a meal with us. We have questions and we will answer all your questions."

Aponi turned to Mondicuet. "Sebastian has asked me about a land called China. I told him I had not heard of it, but that perhaps some of the elders know of it."

Mondicuet said, "I also have not heard of it. I do not think our people have had any contact with a land called China. We know only that to the west of our island are other lands populated by your people, Aponi, and cousins of the Onondaga."

One of the elders sitting nearby, a man of Norse appearance, arose and said, "My name is Balder. My grandfather spoke of the lands to the west. Several of the Norse boats sailed far west into the inland waterways. My grandfather spoke of spending many months in temporary settlements trading with the local people. I do not recall hearing of a land called China. Some of the people they traded with were Onondaga, some were Huron. There were other peoples in that region as well. Some were friendly with the Norse and with one another. Others were hostile. Eventually our Norse explorers left those lands and returned to this island. Eventually most of them returned across the Great Ocean."

Mondicuet said to Sebastian, "The Mikmak, our enemies, damaged the only remaining long boats that the Norse left behind. You will see that our own Beothuk boats are small and not very safe when navigating the rough open water to the west. We stay close to shore where the fish are abundant."

Sebastian paused, then said, "We saw several of the Norse longboats close to the shore, in a rocky area of water. They looked to be damaged, and possibly plagued with rot and vermin. We will examine them and see what can be done. Many of our sailors came aboard with experience in boat building." Smiling at Mondicuet and the others, he continued, "Come with us. Let us feast and get to know one another."

Sebastian turned away as he noticed groups of men and women emerging from several of the small houses. Mondicuet turned toward them, motioned to them to approach, and said to them, "Our visitors have sailed here from the east, across the Great Ocean. They wish to honor us with a feast this very night on the coast. Come! Let us join them."

*   *   *

The group joining Aponi, Balder and Mondicuet and Sebastian numbered close to 30 people. Before they left the village, Mondicuet said to Sebastian, "The rest of our people are hunting; I have sent word to let them know where we have gone."

When the group arrived at the shore, the reaction of all the other villagers accompanying Sebastian and Aponi was astonishment. Two craft larger by far than any other boats they had seen were anchored in the bay. Each had gangplanks that extended to the shore. Men and women went up and down the gangplanks retrieving building materials and personal belongings from the ships. Along the shore groups of men and women were busy at various tasks—some were building shelters; others were excavating a large fire pit; still others were attempting to drag two Norse boats ashore that sat in the rocky area immediately offshore.

Mattea, Erik, Shay and Arne walked up to Sebastian, Aponi, Balder and Mondicuet at the same time. Sebastian introduced Mondicuet. "He is the leader of the local community. They have a wonderful village in a clearing in the midst of this forest. With him is one of the elders named Balder. He has much knowledge of the history of this land."

Mondicuet said to Mattea, "I am honored to meet the mother of this fine young man. He has told me something about your voyage and what you seek." Gazing around at the activities all around them he said, "I see you are preparing a welcome for us. But it is we who should be preparing a welcome for you!"

Mattea smiled, "And so it shall be, but in the morning. Soon there will be meat roasting and drink flowing. We have many questions, as I am sure you do as well."

For the next several hours, Mondicuet and his people assisted in setting up a makeshift dining area. Then, once everyone had settled into the business of eating, the conversations began.

CHAPTER SEVEN

June 1499

The appearance of the damaged Norse boats, along with the stories of the increasing attacks of the Mikmak, had convinced Cabot and his officers that they should organize another series of fortifications like the ones they had constructed to the north. This time they were more experienced and were able to direct the local people more efficiently. Still, Cabot resisted working faster because he wanted to involve and train the local artisans and craftsmen as much as possible.

By the end of that June, he was satisfied that the fortifications would be sufficient to repel any attacks by the Mikmaks. During the process of building the walls, another group of craftsmen, mostly woodworkers from Wales, took on the task of rebuilding the damaged Norse ships. There were three of them, but the damage to them was not as severe as they had feared. Rotten and burned wood was replaced with wood from the cargo on Cabot's ships.

Cabot discussed the defenses of the community in more detail with Mondicuet and other leaders. "Your workers have seen how these boats can be repaired; indeed, the workers can no doubt build several more from wood and materials on hand nearby. How many boats do you think you would need to effectively protect your community?"

Mondicuet said, "These three would be sufficient for the defense of our village here on the coast. But several of us have considered building boats similar to those used by the Mikmak. They are longer, wider, and can travel faster and farther in open seas. We think we could build several over the next few months. With the help of your craftsmen of course!"

"I see. And I take it you're suggesting you would use them to attack your attackers?" Cabot smiled and continued, "Of course we could remain here another few months and help you build those boats. The weather is good. But how long will the weather hold?"

Mondicuet said, "The weather will hold up until the time the sun does not rise until midday. Until then your ships will be safe from ice on the ocean."

Cabot reflected. "It would probably take three or four months for us to help you construct several boats like the Mikmak use. What would the weather be like at that time?"

"That would take you into winter. You could not possibly depart when the seas are full of ice." Cabot wasn't sure whether he detected a half-smile on Mondicuet's face when he said that.

The conversation paused for a few moments. Mattea, who had been listening nearby, approached and asked, "When you speak of the ocean, will there be only open seas, or will we pass land?"

Mondicuet said, "Our elders spoke of a voyage of perhaps a week between this island and a great land mass to the west. And they made that voyage in long boats similar to those you see here. In your huge ships, you might make the voyage in much less time. Balder's grandfather was one of those who made that voyage and he often spoke of it."

October 1499 to March 1500

Cabot and the other officers decided they would not risk sailing into ice-bound waters, waters that were unknown to them. They would wait til spring, and made their temporary camp a more semipermanent home. The Beothuk communities were greatly relieved at their decision.

During that time Cabot's crews worked more diligently on improving the living conditions in the area. He assigned several crew members skilled in carpentry to assist the local craftsmen in building stronger, larger and more weather-resistant houses.

Because the Beothuk communities were occasionally attacked by the Mikmak in their ocean-going boats, Cabot suggested building boats similar to those of the Mikmak. The response to his suggestion was enthusiastic, and the carpentry teams Cabot had set up soon expanded into a boat-building operation.

Mondicuet approached Cabot as the ship-building crews were finishing construction of the last of the five Mikmak boats. "Captain, I have been thinking that the defense of our island perhaps would be more effective if it began at the source of the trouble—the north of the island, directly across from the Mikmak land."

Cabot looked intrigued. "Are you suggesting that a crew of your people would take several of these boats to the north of the island and present them to your brethren there?"

"Yes, and the crew would be composed of those who had the most experience in the building of these boats. That way our brethren in the north could embark on a boat-building operation using plans that had been perfected here."

Cabot sighed and smiled. "I think that's an excellent idea. And I would suggest you store on board a number of clay fire pots full of pitch. They make very effective weapons when set afire and hurled at a target. We can teach you how to make simple catapults that would enable you to send the fire pots much farther than simply throwing them by hand."

Mondicuet nodded, then added. "I have another suggestion; it's not related to the Mikmak issue. Aponi has expressed her wish to perhaps join you on your voyage to lands west of here. As you know, she was born and raised in those lands but came to live with us at the age of 10. She has strong memories of her homeland and still remembers the language of her people. She also recalls the route her people took when they sailed here. In addition to Aponi, a Norse elder in our community, Balder, wishes to accompany you. His memory of those waters would supplement Aponi's memory. Aponi's stepfather, Dogajavik, will remain on the island with his community. He perhaps does not feel the urge to explore new lands at his age."

April 1500

Dawn was lightening the sky as the two English ships and two of the newly constructed "Mikmak boats" were being loaded with supplies and crew in the harbor. The six Beothuks who had accompanied Cabot's ships on the voyage south—the women Gwinya, Abidish and Cosweet, and the men Gobidin, Kooreh, and Matuis—were boarding the Mikmak boats. Two men and one woman would be in each of the two boats.

Cabot explained that for the first part of the journey, the English ships would sail north along the island with their two new Mikmak boats sailing alongside. As they came within view of the huge mainland to their north, the Mikmak boats would continue hugging their island's coastline and Cabot's two ships would turn west looking for the land of China.

When the ships were ready to depart, Cabot addressed their Beothuk guests and elaborated on his earlier announcement: "At the point our boats reach the latitude where Balder and Aponi say there will be a large island to our west, our English ships will depart from you. They do not believe the island will be visible at that point. But Aponi tells me that she recalls the behavior of the currents and the sea birds that mark the approach to it. Both she and Balder say there will be a channel to the north of the island, a channel that separates the island from a large landmass to the north.

"We on the two English ships shall make for that channel. You Beothuk on the Mikmak boats shall continue sailing north along the coast of your land until you reach your destination. We, the crews and captains and guests, wish you success in your defense of your lands against the Mikmak."

CHAPTER EIGHT

Portugal—May, 1500

Father Martim Rodrigo awoke in his bedroom in the Church of Santa Clara, Oporto, Portugal. Actually, he wasn't entirely sure he was awake. He had spent almost the whole day before in a state of shock and went to bed early. The day before that was when he created a new future for his beloved Portugal.

Father Rodrigo forced himself to get up. He called for his housekeeper to prepare his breakfast. Then he remembered with a shock—he no longer had a housekeeper. He had no servants at all. Have I ever had servants? Didn't there used to be slaves working for the Church?

The change to his world had occurred in an instant. The memory of that instant still reverberated in Rodrigo's consciousness. He reminded himself that it was his spherical astrolabe that created this new world, an astrolabe modified by the famous, some would say infamous, Parisian alchemist Nicolas Flamel.

Father Rodrigo thought back to the time, many years ago, when he was parish priest in Mogadishu, Somalia. One of his parishioners had obtained a broken spherical astrolabe and presented it to the "Great Admiral" Vasco da Gama, who was exploring the Indian Ocean for the Portuguese king. The parishioner explained that the astrolabe would be an invaluable tool to ensure da Gama's success in rounding the treacherous southern tip of Africa, the Cape of Good Hope, which was much more treacherous going from east to west than the other direction.

Father Rodrigo, who was planning to retire from his post as parish priest, asked to accompany da Gama on his return voyage to Portugal, and da Gama granted the request. Then da Gama surprised Rodrigo by gifting the astrolabe back to him.

What da Gama didn't know—indeed, almost nobody knew – was that the astrolabe was more than a device for navigating the oceans, which was all the Great Admiral thought it was. Years before, it had been modified by Flamel and turned into a time machine, what Flamel lovingly described as "a device for navigating the interstices of time itself!"

Father Rodrigo wasn't worried that da Gama would discover the true capabilities of the astrolabe. A wire inside the device had broken and couldn't be repaired with the technologies and tools that were then available in Mogadishu.

Rodrigo would happily have left the broken astrolabe in a museum somewhere, and never thought about it again, had he not discovered a terrible truth about his beloved homeland, Portugal. When Rodrigo returned to Portugal upon his retirement after 40 years as a church pastor in Mogadishu, he discovered that slavery had become widespread throughout Portugal and its colonies. Portuguese mariners had coerced West African communities to sell people to the Portuguese, who transported them as slaves to Europe and the New World.

It was then that Father Rodrigo had decided to try to prevent that from ever happening—in other words, by going back in time, before slavery began, and preventing it from ever occurring. He managed to have the spherical astrolabe repaired by his friend Gabriel Hugo, a Parisian jeweler who now lived in Oporto and specialized in repairing intricate watches and clocks.

Rodrigo then convinced his three Malian servants who had been presented to the church as slaves to use the machine to transport themselves 60 years back in time and break the chain of events that created the slavery network from Africa to the New World.

The plan worked! Actually, Father Rodrigo only learned— indirectly—that the plan worked after his Malian servants were transported to the past and put the plan in motion. He discovered, as soon as he awoke the next morning, that Portugal had become a changed country. It was as if slavery had never existed in Portugal. Not only that, but Portugal, with its once-booming Portuguese economy previously stimulated by the slave trade and colonialism, was now an economic backwater.

Father Rodrigo knew that no matter who he talked to about the change, he would be regarded as crazy. In everyone's mind, there had never been slavery in Portugal. Foremost in everyone's mind was the current state of war with Spain.

Rodrigo's motivation to change history had been rooted in his belief that only a war between those rivals would prevent the slave trade from evolving. Spain and Portugal would be too preoccupied in defending themselves to develop the slave trade. Rodrigo formulated a plan and enlisted Hugo and the three sisters in his plan. They would prepare the astrolabe for its voyage back in time. The plan worked perfectly.

Upon the sisters' arrival back in time to Mali, the first step in the plan was for them to convince the ruler to sail a fleet of pirogues to the islands a few hours off the West African coast. Knowing in advance precisely when European explorers would "discover" the islands, the Malians would take them prisoner and seize their caravels.

Once the Malians learned to sail the caravels, they would create a naval force from the captured ships. First disguising them as Spanish ships, the Malian navy would sail to Portugal, destroy the major ports, and seize some of their caravels. Then the Malian navy would retreat back into the Great Ocean, change their markings to those of Portugal, sail into the Spanish ports, and do the same thing to them.

On the first morning after the sisters were sent back in time, Father Rodrigo learned from his contacts in the Portuguese and Spanish churches what was happening to their respective ports. The complaints and questions were the same in all the churches—We don't understand why this is happening! Which government started this war?

But Rodrigo knew why it was happening. And he knew who the actual attackers were—it was naval forces from Mali, the country to which the spherical astrolabe had transported the three Malian sisters. It wasn't the Spanish Navy that was attacking the Portuguese ports, and it wasn't the Portuguese Navy that was attacking the Spanish ports. The attackers were the government of Mali and its allies in the New World who were determined to prevent Portugal and Spain from stealing Africans and using them in their brutal colonization plans. It would appear our plan has been carried out. I only wish I could learn more of the details from an eyewitness… or a participant!

*   *   *

Father Rodrigo dressed and went into the kitchen to make his breakfast. He decided to eat in the courtyard to enjoy the birdsong and breezes. After half an hour contemplating his new world, he was surprised to see his old friend Gabriel enter the courtyard.

"Ah, my Parisian co-conspirator in our breathtaking plan, the master jeweler Gabriel Hugo! How are you?"

Gabriel put down his cane and sat in the chair opposite Father Rodrigo. He looked confused as he stared at the priest. Then he said, "What have we done, Father? This is not the world we inhabited two days ago!" He paused, took a breath, and continued, "But it seems to be a better world, wouldn't you agree?"

"Indeed, I do agree. But I am a little concerned about this war."

Gabriel nodded, but then said, "At least it is only the ships in the ports the Malians are attacking, not the cities."

The priest raised his eyebrows, put his finger to his lips and said, "You mustn't say that where others might overhear you."

"You are right. Forgive me." In a low voice he added, "In any event, even if the Spanish and Portuguese monarchies might wish to launch attacks on one another's cities, they do not have the resources to do so. They have not yet stolen the wealth of the Americas with which they could have financed such attacks on one another. And, we can hope and pray, they never will."

Father Rodrigo waited for his friend to catch his breath before responding. "So, my friend, Master Hugo, what brings you to my humble abode? As you have no doubt noticed, my abode is a lot humbler than it was last week!"

Gabriel chuckled and then turned serious. He said, "Martim, when I awoke this morning, I saw that someone had left this at my home. It's a note from Nicolas Flamel, my former employer. Here, I'll let you read it aloud."

Father Rodrigo took the note, unrolled it and read it: "My dear friend Gabriel. I need you to return to Europe, Paris in particular. I will meet you there at my home. I have neglected events that will soon occur in England, events that I should have remembered from my previous travels to the future. And the need is urgent.

"You, my old friend and former apprentice, must convince our good priest Father Rodrigo into joining you! I trust you will believe me when I tell you that this matter is of the utmost importance!

"I can only say at this time that the matter concerns the upcoming marriage between Prince Arthur, the heir-apparent of King Henry the Seventh of England, and young Princess Catherine of Aragon. Arthur is in grave danger, although he does not suspect it yet. I alone know of the danger, its cause, and its historic result. Historic, unless we— you and I and Father Rodrigo—can avert the danger.

"You no doubt believe it will not be possible to have any

influence on those events in England. Do not worry. At this moment, or soon hereafter, Captain John Cabot's English fleet will make landfall in the New World on the island of Guanahani and will encounter Captain Janaina Watu and her officers Ibrahim and Musa of the Malian Federation Navy. Those two officers are the 38-year-old twin sons of Maryam, your former slave, who married Yousef, one of the freed African slaves. I have sent word to Captain Janaina asking her to convince Captain John Cabot and his fleet to return from the Malian naval base in Guanahani to Paris. Please, please, honor her request. I beg of you! Again, my colleague Janaina will explain everything."

Rodrigo handed the note back to his friend. He looked up at Hugo. "I take it you are intrigued by Master Flamel's entreaty." Then Rodrigo got up from the table, walked to the garden wall and looked out at the cobblestone streets in the distance. Turning around, he said to Gabriel, "My friend, there is nothing for me here in Oporto any longer. Let us journey to Paris!"

CHAPTER NINE

October 1500

Mattea was having a terrible time sleeping; or rather dreaming. It wasn't a matter of seasickness. She had never been plagued by that during her voyages with John from Genoa, to Spain, to France, to England and on this voyage across the Atlantic Ocean. By all accounts, she should have been having a relaxing, eye-opening experience as the two ships continued their westward voyage, encountering beautiful islands and inlets, some inhabited, some uninhabited, some barren, some lush.

No, something else was interfering with her dreams. She complained to her husband about them. "John, the dreams are bizarre and often featuring the same people and story!"

Cabot set down the map he was drawing of the voyage so far. "Earlier you had dreamt of ships with African crews and female crews. More of those dreams?"

"Some of that, but even stranger. In addition to Africans and women sailing the ship, there were two men who appeared to be a priest and some kind of mysterious magician or wizard. The two men were discussing a nautical device that the mysterious man called a 'spherical astrolabe.'"

Cabot's attention became more focused. "A spherical astrolabe?

51

I've heard of such a device. I wish I had one for our voyage. Did these two men talk much about the device?"

"No, not much, only that they planned to dispose of it. They seemed to think it was dangerous."

Cabot chuckled and said, "Well, I hardly think a spherical astrolabe could be considered dangerous. On the contrary, a sea voyage without one would be more dangerous than a voyage with one." He paused and said, "I envy your ability to recall your dreams in such detail; even conversations! I rarely remember any of my dreams, let alone conversations." Then he smiled and gestured toward the paperwork on his desk. "Forgive me, my dear. But I need to finish my chart. Let me know if you have more of those dreams."

Mattea nodded and smiled. "I'll help you with the charts whenever you like. Just let me know." Then she kissed her husband on the cheek, turned and walked out of their captain's cabin. She paused at the rail. She turned back to Cabot and said, "John, Sebastian is signaling us from his ship."

Cabot set down his map, stood and walked outside to the rail. "Yes, his signal says for us to follow his ship into the waterway between that land mass on our right and this island on our left."

Aponi also saw the signal and came up to Cabot and Mattea. "I recognize that waterway! That is where our little Onondaga fleet emerged when we ventured on our ill-fated voyage to the land of the Beothuk and Mikmak people. In the Mohawk language it is called 'Kaniataro Wanenneh.' That means 'Big Waterway'."

Mattea said, "I cannot see beyond the mouth, or what appears to be a mouth. Is it a channel between two land masses? Or is it the mouth of a bay?"

Aponi said, "I was very young at the time and I had not accompanied the explorations of the waterway to the west. I believe it is the mouth of a bay. Although whether the mouth emerges from a lake or a river, I do not know."

Balder had overheard their conversation and joined in. "I have a better memory of that waterway. It is the mouth of a broad river that emerges from a lake several days' journey to the west. But the expedition my people were on didn't penetrate much farther than the lake. The people we encountered and dealt with told us there were other bodies of water to the west of that, but I have no memory of them."

Cabot looked up, interested. "I'm happy to hear that the Norse had friendly encounters with the people along that waterway, for we shall soon be in the middle of it!"

After a few hours, the sailors could see settlements on both shores of the river and on large islands in the middle of the river. Captain Cabot made a quick announcement to his pilot. "I'm sure you can see that group of people on the northern shore. They appear to be motioning us to enter that small bay just to the west. It looks like a harbor of a large village. Make for the harbor!"

Once again, as the ships had done earlier upon entering a bay of unknown depth, two sailors lowered a ship's boat, rowed it into the bay and took measurements using a rope weighted by large pieces of lead every fathom. Mattea reported the results, "John, it appears the bay is deep enough for our ships to enter safely."

Cabot gave the order for the two ships to enter and drop anchor near the shore. Once Cabot and the other officers had made sure the anchorages were secure, the crews began going ashore in the ships' boats; some of the younger crew members chose to swim ashore. Aponi eagerly dove from a ship and joined the swimmers.

The scene that awaited the sailors was astounding. In the far distance, they could see a shimmering group of buildings, or at least their images. In front of that vision, about 100 yards from the shoreline, was a group of some 25 to 30 people—men and women. Aponi was not surprised that they appeared to be Iroquois, Onondaga or Huron. They wore leggings of the type she knew was common among those people. Even their physical characteristics resembled hers—black hair, reddish/tan skin, tall athletic build.

Three of the people on shore—two men and one woman—detached themselves from the group and approached the visitors. They scanned the crews until they stopped at the sight of Aponi. The woman addressed Aponi directly in Onondaga, "Welcome, sister from our nations." She stepped forward, crossed her hands on her chest, and bowed slightly.

Aponi smiled and said, "Your welcome fills our hearts with joy. I am Aponi." Pointing to Cabot she said, "This is John Cabot, Captain of the larger ship, a carrack. He is from England, on the eastern shore of the Great Ocean." Pointing to Arne, she said, "This is Captain Arne of the smaller ship, a caravel. He is a Norseman, also from across the Great Ocean." She turned to Cabot and said to him, "I will translate for you. I do not think the people speak Norse or any other language of Europe."

But to her surprise and to everyone else's, one of the men replied in Norse. "I do not think language will prove to be a problem." Then he introduced himself and his companions. "I am Ayenwatha, ambassador of the Onondaga Nation." Pointing to the woman beside him he said, "This is Jikonhassee. She is known as the `Mother of the Nations'."

Finally, and with great dignity, Ayenwatha introduced the other man. "This is Tekahawi'ta, the Great Peacemaker. It was he who gave birth to the idea of what all the peoples in this region have created, the Haudenosaunee Confederacy. It is he who will join all our peoples with those of Quetzalcóatl, the Feathered Serpent of the western lands!"

A sudden silence descended on the visitors at Ayenwatha's words. Tekahawi'ta smiled at Aponi. He let his gaze drift over the assembled sailors, then nodded at Ayenwatha. Ayenwatha smiled, stepped forward, and spoke to Mattea directly, "Come, tell us your name and allow us to escort you and your company to our Welcome House."

To Mattea's astonishment, her apprehension evaporated, and she said, "I am Mattea, wife of Captain John Cabot standing beside me, whom our guest Aponi has introduced already. I am from the land of Venezia in Europe. My husband is from the land of Genoa in Europe."

Cabot bowed and said, "My wife and I are honored by your greeting. The others in our crew are from other lands in Europe. We will accept your invitation and look forward to forming a bond of friendship with your people."

Cabot turned to the rest of the crews assembled on the shore and said, "Follow us. We will be guests of this noble nation!"

It took some time for the crews of the two ships to assemble and approach the small group on shore. At a signal from Ayenwatha the group of Onondagas turned and began walking slowly away from the shore and toward the grassland. The glimmering vision of a village in the distance became more distinct. The village made such an impression on Mattea that she never forgot her first reaction. She described its appearance in great detail in her journal afterward:

"The village is circular and is completely enclosed by a wooden palisade in three tiers like a pyramid. The top one is built crosswise, the middle one perpendicular and the lowest one of strips of wood placed lengthwise. The whole is well joined and lashed together after their manner, and is some two lances in height. There is only one gate and entrance to this village, and that can be barred up. Over this gate and in many places about the enclosure are species of galleries with ladders for mounting to them, which galleries are provided with rocks and stones for defense and protection of the place. There are some fifty houses in this village, each about fifty or more paces in length, and twelve or fifteen in width, built completely of wood and covered in and bordered up with large pieces of bark and rind of trees, as broad as a table, which are well and cunningly lashed after their manner. And inside these houses are many rooms and chambers; and in the middle is a large space without a floor, where they light their fire and live together in common."

Ayenwatha stood in the doorway of the Welcome House, which was a modest one-story structure directly in front of the wooden palisade that surrounded the village. Arrayed in the ground in front of the Welcome House were several dozen carpets of woven grasses and branches intended for sitting and resting. Ayenwatha smiled and gestured for Mattea, Cabot, Sebastian, Arne, Balder and Aponi to enter the Welcome House. "You six may sit with us inside. Your crews are too numerous to join us inside, but they may make themselves comfortable on the carpets. We shall have some food and drink brought to them. You six may join us for food and drink inside as we discuss your presence in our land."

When the six invitees entered Welcome House, they were shown seats at a large round table. Ayenwatha followed and asked them to be seated. He then motioned for Jikonhassee and Tekahawi'ta to come to the table. Once the six guests were seated, their hosts took their seats.

Ayenwatha said, "Six months before your arrival there was a fluctuation in history. The fluctuation was a deviation from the former history's path. Our Prophet, the Great Peacemaker was the first to perceive this fluctuation. He will now help us understand how this fluctuation came about and what result is unfolding before our eyes."

Ayenwatha turned to Jikonhassee and nodded. Jikonhassee stood and walked to a large doorway in front of which hung a magnificent tapestry of many colors. She carefully moved aside the tapestry and disappeared through the doorway. A moment later she emerged carrying a long silver rod around which were wound five groups of threads. She set them on the table, then turned to Captain Cabot and said, "Each of the threads is a pathway to a future you might enter. You must tell us of your journey and your goals, and after that, the Great Peacemaker, Tekahawi'ta, will select the correct group of threads."

Cabot: "Our journey is to the land called China. Do you know of it? Is it nearby? We are on a trading mission and seek to establish friendship between China and our nation."

Jikonhassee looked puzzled. She said, "I know of no land called China. To the west of where we are is a vast continent. The people are like us. It is not called China."

Tekahawi'ta nodded and spoke directly to Captain Cabot, "The land you seek you will not reach on your present voyage. It is far distant, on the other side of our world. But I see a different purpose in your voyage, one that will bring together all the nations of this side of our world." He stood and walked to the table. Turning back to face Cabot he said, "I will select the threads of your true voyage and we will learn where they lead."

Turning back to the silver rod, Tekahawi'ta reached out and gently separated the groups of threads into their respective colors: red, yellow, brown, white and black. He gently stroked the threads of each color group silently. He put his arms down and stood silently in meditation.

After a few moments, he turned to the group and said, "Your journey will lead you to peoples of all these colors. Indeed, you have already encountered peoples of the white, red and yellow colors on your journey to our lands. But you have yet to encounter peoples of the black and brown colors. You will soon do so."

Mattea was startled at Tekahawi'ta's words. She spoke to him. "Master, in my dreams I have encountered such peoples—black and brown peoples. They spoke different languages to one another but not to me. I was on their ship upon the Great Ocean. I did not understand their speech, but I believed some of them spoke Arabic."

"Arabic; yes. That leads me to talk to you about the fluctuation I see in these threads." Tekahawi'ta turned back to the threads on the table. Selecting one of the white threads, he turned and spoke to Mattea and John. "Your king will die in nine years. His older son will become king. Because of this fluctuation I see in these threads, that son will not die in your lifetime, and his younger brother will therefore not carry out his disastrous destiny, a destiny he owned before history fluctuated and saved itself."

Tekahawi'ta was silent for a few moments before resuming. "The older son, once he becomes the new king, will become your ally when you enter the stream of the fluctuation." He paused again and said, "But the journey you are on now, a journey that will carry you to the stream of the new history, will challenge you many times. Just know this... it will not desert you."

Tekahawi'ta put down the threads and gazed out over the room, acknowledging each of the guests with a smile. "It is time for us to enjoy a meal. Then an early end to this glorious day. Tomorrow you will continue your journey; but not to the west. No, your destiny lies to the south."

*   *   *

After their meal that evening, Captain Cabot and Mattea called a meeting of the ships' officers to discuss their plans. "Gentlemen, we have heard Tekahawi'ta talk of our location and our journey. What are your thoughts?"

Arne spoke first. "At first, I was not inclined to believe him when he said we could not reach China on our present route. But something about the man convinced me that he speaks the truth. He counsels us to proceed south and follow the contour of this continent."

Mattea nodded and said, "I agree with Tekahawi'ta's advice. I believe he tells the truth about our journey. We should return out of this river and proceed south along the coast. What do you say, John?"

Cabot was silent for a moment before answering. "I suppose Tekahawi'ta was confirming what you experienced in your dreams—that we would encounter brown and black people, even people who speak Arabic." He was silent for a few more moments and then said,

"What do we have to lose? If we keep land in sight as we sail south, we shall meet our destiny. Whatever that destiny will turn out to be."

*   *   *

The next day the crews and officers occupied themselves with preparations for their journey. They spent one more night as guests of the Haudenosaunee Confederacy and replenished their ships' supplies before taking their leave at dawn's first light. Balder and Aponi had decided to stay with the expedition to see what might await them.

The following two days were spent emerging from the Kaniataro Wanenneh, the Onondaga name meaning "Big Waterway," and skirting around several islands before the ships were able to sail in a more-or-less southerly direction. Cabot was intent on not losing sight of land to their west.

CHAPTER TEN

June, 1501, Guanahani

Cabot was glad to be on solid land once again. The voyage during the past six months had been one of open ocean with very few opportunities to make landfall; at least not landfall on the mainland of the huge continent his ships were passing to the west. They had been warned that the many groups of people on the mainland might not welcome them, so Cabot restricted his landings to the small islands off shore. At least that way they were able to replenish their stocks of food and fresh water, as well as give the crews a chance to get off the ships and onto solid ground for a few hours.

When his ships had traveled 1,700 nautical miles south, a group of islands came into view. Cabot determined the coordinates to be approximately 22 degrees north latitude and 74 degrees west longitude. He decided his crew deserved a time to rest on land. He ordered the two ships to determine the depth of a large circular bay. When it was determined to be deep enough for the ships to enter, they did so.

Once the two ships were firmly at anchor, the crews wasted no time disembarking, bathing and walking on the beach. Captain Cabot counseled his crews not to penetrate beyond the line of trees at the end of the beach. "We don't know what lies beyond, whether it be wild animals, swamp, or dangerous people. Stay close for a while."

Sebastian was the first to notice the people emerging from the trees. "Father, it appears we have visitors." Cabot, Mattea and their two other sons turned to face the tree line and saw a group of two men, two women and four children standing near the trees staring at the sailors and the ships. Their clothing appeared to be European.

The two men began walking toward the sailors and halted when they were within speaking distance. The taller of the two spoke first, "Hail, visitors from Europe! We see by your ships' markings and flags that you come from England."

Mattea was astonished. "John, they're speaking Spanish! And they look Spanish as well. How can that be?" Before Cabot could answer, the other six people in the group began walking toward the sailors. When they stood next to the two Spaniards, they spoke to them in a strange language.

The taller of the two Spaniards answered them in that language and then turned back to address Mattea. "Madam, you are correct. We two are originally from Spain. The others you see with us are our wives and sons. Our wives are Taino people. Our sons are mixed Spanish and Taino. I was speaking to them in the Taino language."

The other Spaniard spoke. "I am Geraldo. My brother here is Carlos. Our wives are Jin and Siba, the boys are Guabasa, Bayamo, Hatuey and Bana."

Cabot spoke. "Greetings to you! You are correct that our voyage began in England. I am Captain John Cabot and this is my wife, Ship's Officer Mattea Jacobella. This is Captain Arne of the larger ship you see at anchor. Our son Sebastian is his First Mate. We are seeking trade relations with the noble people of this land." Cabot paused, then continued. "Did you say you come from Spain? How so? With whom? We Europeans have heard of the Great Explorer Cristoforo Colombo. Sad to say, all of Europe was grieved to learn that his fleet was lost as he voyaged to search for China."

Carlos looked at Geraldo, smiled and turned back to answer Cabot. "Noble Captain and Madame Jacobella, we are aware of that story. But thanks be to God and the Malian Federation, the story is not true. Our Master Colombo's fleet survived. It landed on this island nine years ago."

Cabot was stunned into silence. Mattea took a deep breath and spoke to Carlos. "Sir, pardon our questions, but what you say puzzles us. We have seen no sign of a Spanish fleet on this island or indeed anywhere nearby. Nor have we heard of the Malian Federation. Does it have to do with the Kingdom of Mali, in Africa?"

Carlos smiled, "Yes, indeed, the Malian Federation originated in the Kingdom of Mali. But it is widespread, on both sides of the Atlantic Ocean." He turned to Geraldo and nodded.

At that point Geraldo spoke. "Captain and Madame, your arrival was anticipated. And we have prepared a fitting reception for your noble crews." Turning, Geraldo pointed to the far end of the bay and said, "Beyond the end of this bay is an entrance to another bay. A much larger, but hidden, bay. A ship from the Malian Federation sits at anchor in that bay. Our modest city sits on the far side of that hidden bay. Come! Let us answer your questions and provide you with food, drink and rest. Captain Cabot, I will come aboard your ship and guide you to the hidden entrance. Your son's ship may follow."

John, Mattea and Sebastian agreed and informed the ships' crews to reboard the vessels and prepare to raise anchor.

*   *   *

It took almost an hour for the sailors to get out of the water, reboard their ships, and raise anchor. Geraldo joined Mattea and John on the carrack Le Michel and guided them to the end of the bay. They could just barely discern what looked like the entrance to another bay behind a small island. Geraldo said, "It's not an island at all, just a floating raft of greenery disguised to look like an island." He asked Shay to lower a small boat. Then he and Geraldo climbed in it and rowed to the floating island. Geraldo grabbed hold of a bush and directed Shay to row the boat away from the entrance. Once that was done, a much larger bay became visible. Geraldo released the floating island some distance away from the entrance to the bay. The two men then rowed back to Le Michel and reboarded.

Shay reported to Cabot that the entrance to the larger bay appeared large enough for a large ship to enter. Cabot gave the order for the ships to enter the bay.

The sailors were astonished at what they saw. The bay was mostly circular and ringed with houses, docks and piers. There were people walking about on land, on the docks, and farther away from the shore in front of houses and other buildings. But an equally astonishing sight was that of a large caravel floating at anchor near the longest pier. Emblazoned on sides of the ship were the words "Malian-Quonambec Federation."

Captains Cabot and Arne guided their ships to where Geraldo had indicated they could drop anchor and prepare for disembarkation. The captains ordered the ships' boats lowered, and the crews began going ashore.

Once everyone was ashore, their surprise at seeing what looked like a good-sized village became an even bigger surprise when they got a closer look at the people. Mattea put her hand on her husband's shoulder and said, "John, look! There are European people here, and African people! And the other people are different from them— brown complexion, straight black hair! What a land we have come to!"

Cabot and Arne directed their crews to assemble in a grassy area a short distance from the shore. As the sailors walked that distance, they were greeted by smiling people, some of whom spoke to them in languages they didn't understand. Geraldo smiled at the people, then said to Mattea, "As I said earlier, we've been expecting you. Please have a seat on the grass and make yourselves comfortable." Then he pointed to the caravel and said, "It looks like the captain and her officers are coming over to greet and welcome you!"

A tall, bronze-complexioned woman with black hair strode towards them. She wore what looked like some kind of uniform with the words "Malian-Quonambec Federation" printed on the left side of a short jacket. Accompanying her were two men who appeared to be African. When the three of them reached the sailors, they stopped. Cabot, Arne, Sebastian, Shay and Mattea stood up and faced them.

The woman smiled and said, "Welcome, Captain Cabot! This is our community of Guanahani. And Madame Jacobella, you are doubly welcomed! The first woman ship's officer to cross the Great Ocean!" Turning to Cabot's officers, she said, "Welcome to you both."

Then she addressed the group as a whole, "I am Captain Janaina Watu and these are my two ship's Officers, Ibrahim and Musa." She smiled at the puzzled looks of the sailors. "Yes, I understand. You are puzzled. You see African people here. You see people of the New World here. I will explain. But first, would you like to come inside our Welcome House? I'm sure you would be more comfortable, and I would guess you are hungry for real food! Come, let us go inside."

Mattea smiled, but then said, "I'm not sure why, but I feel comfortable with your invitation. And I'm certainly tired of being on board a ship." Turning to Cabot and the others, she said, "Well, shall we accept Captain Watu's invitation?"

There was no objection. With quite a few groans, sighs and chuckles, the group of sailors arose and began walking to the Welcome House. It was a very large structure of trees, planks and stone. From the outside, it appeared large enough to easily accommodate more than 100 people.

Inside there were six very long wooden tables with benches running along their length on both sides. The aroma of roasted meat and maize filled the room. Captain Janaina said, "Please, everyone, take a seat. We shall have a meal and then I will explain why you are here and what lies ahead for you."

*   *   *

A meal of questions and answers

The officers and mates were too famished to begin asking the questions that otherwise would have occupied their minds. But those questions eventually fought their way to the surface.

Mattea was the first to stand and address Captain Janaina. "We are overwhelmed by your generosity. But even more overwhelmed are we by the many strange events we have witnessed these past few months. First, we encounter, not China, but Onondaga people and people of the Haudenosaunee Confederacy, people who inhabit a great river leading into a vast continent. The leader of those peoples—actually, there appeared to be three leaders—told us we would encounter people farther down the southern coasts. And here we have… I do not know where to begin."

Janaina spoke, "And you are also puzzled by what seems to be our foreknowledge of your arrival. That is understandable. I will tell you what I know, but I will not be surprised if you have trouble believing my story. But please, please, understand that I have no desire to deceive you. What I tell you will perhaps convince you. But what I am about to say is of the utmost importance to your world and our world."

Janaina paused. She gazed about the large dining hall. Then she turned back to Mattea. "Madame Jacobella, first allow me to explain who our people are. This group of islands—indeed, this entire landmass west of the Great Ocean—is the ancestral home of people like me, Taino and Arawak peoples. Other people you see here—people from Africa and Europe—came here as you came here. Well, not precisely the way you came here. Some—the people from Europe—came here as explorers such as yourselves. Others—the people from Africa—came here as prisoners and slaves of the European explorers. The explorers were primarily from Portugal and Spain, and were bent on discovering the vast continent of China.

"Of course, as you have learned, this is not the vast continent of China."

Janaina paused and gestured to Ibrahim and Musa, asking them to stand. "These two men are my First Officers. Their parents were Africans—Maryam and Yousef, from the African empire of Mali."

She motioned for them to come over to where she was standing. She smiled and said to one of them, "Musa, why don't you tell our guests about your parents?"

Musa nodded, smiled at Mattea and the others, and began his story. "My father, Yousef, was taken as a slave from the interior of Mali. He was stolen by the Portuguese and made to work on a ship that sailed the Atlantic Ocean. That ship was one of three ships caught in a storm that blew them to what some people call the Cabo Verde Islands. I will shorten my story a bit and just say that the islands were NOT uninhabited. The people who lived on those islands were Africans, including my mother, Maryam, and her two sisters Khadijah and Sofia."

Musa paused and resumed, "Now... I hope you'll not be too impatient for a full explanation of that history. I promise that you will learn that history. But for now, there is a matter of critical importance that you must attend to. I'll let my brother Ibrahim explain that."

Musa sat down, smiled, and waited for his brother to stand and take up the tale. Ibrahim laughed and said, "My brother bravely left it to me to regale you with the most entangled and fantastic part of our tale. A tale you might be inclined to disbelieve, but bear with me."

Ibrahim continued, "Let me first go right to the most important point. Your beloved monarch, King Henry, the seventh of his line with that name, is ill. It is now June in the year 1501 according to your Christian calendar. King Henry has less than eight years to live before he will die due to a lung disease.

"Of equally critical importance is that his anointed heir, Prince Arthur—according to the history that we must attempt to change—will die on April 2, 1502, six months after his marriage to Princess Caterina of Spain. The history of which I speak told of him falling ill with a mysterious sweating sickness at England's Ludlow Castle and dying soon afterwards."

Mattea signaled her wish to respond. "Captain Janaina, you speak of a history in which these events took place. How could such a history exist, let alone be accurate, since it lies in the future?"

Janaina smiled, sighed and then said, "The answer to your question will be explained by the man who foresaw that history, a man named Nicolas Flamel from Paris. Many of our people are acquainted with Monsieur Flamel. He will await you in Paris some six months from now. He will explain his plan for you to travel to England to warn the prince."

Cabot said, "You ask us to return to Europe. To Paris, and then to England. To meet with this mysterious man who you say has seen the future, and then meet with Crown Prince Arthur." He paused, looked around at their hosts, and resumed, "Even if we agreed to your plan, why would Arthur agree to meet with us? For that matter, if he did agree to meet with us, what could we possibly tell him that would convince him we were not crazy?"

Janaina said, "Well, in the first place, your voyage to this New World, as you call it, will not result in any amount of trading success. Our people do not have 'goods,' as you are no doubt hoping to obtain. Our people are simple, almost primitive people. They grow food, make simple dwellings and boats, and raise animals. They do not make trade goods, surely not goods that would interest Europeans. There are no valuable minerals in our lands.

"That being said, a return to Europe will be in your best interests. And as I said, your return will set in motion events that we hope will reverse a very dangerous situation."

Cabot resumed his questioning. "You have not explained why the prince would meet with us, or what we would discuss with him."

Janaina said, "This is the plan we suggest. First you will meet with the king to present your report to him. You will inform him that a new world exists on the western side of the Atlantic Ocean; it is not China, which lies on the far western side of the new world. But besides presenting your report to King Henry, which I am sure he will receive with grave attention, you will ask his leave to attend the wedding of his eldest son, Arthur. That will be your most important task."

Mattea interjected, "Why will that be the most important task? Does it have to do with your so-called prophecy of his death?"

"Exactly. Of course, you will not simply warn him of the prophecy. He would dismiss you as a foolish soothsayer, or worse. No, you will congratulate Arthur and present him and his bride, Catherine of Aragon, with matching rings."

Mattea frowned. "Rings? How will that prevent his death, as you have predicted?"

Janaina smiled. "The rings will have a property of promoting vigor and health. Most importantly, the gems on those rings will be capable of preventing many types of disease. That is their purpose—to counteract the sweating sickness he will be exposed to."

"Who has such rings? What substance are they made of?"

"A very skilled jeweler, Gabriel Hugo, will make them and have them ready in Paris at the home of Nicolas Flamel. From there, Father Rodrigo and Gabriel Hugo will join your passengers as your ships return to England."

Mattea said, "You haven't told me what the rings are made of."

Janaina said, "I will leave that to Messieurs Hugo and Flamel. The description of the rings and their properties is beyond me, I'm afraid."

Mattea turned to John. "Well, my captain and my husband. What do you think of Janaina's suggestion for the rest of our journey."

Captain Cabot turned to his men, who were sitting patiently, satiated. Cabot was silent for a few moments. Then he asked Arne, Sebastian and Shay, "What are your thoughts? Shall we abandon our original purpose and return to Europe? According to our host, the preservation of Arthur's life is of utmost importance. Should he die, and his younger brother become king, our host says a series of disasters will ensue. Even if her prediction should not come about, her description of the absence of trade possibilities in this hemisphere seems reason enough to return to England."

Arne answered, "The three of us have been listening to Captain Janaina Watu's proposal and are also inclined to follow her advice."

CHAPTER ELEVEN

Father Rodrigo and Gabriel Hugo were ready to begin their journey soon after receiving Flamel's letter. It took them less than two months to get their affairs in order. The priest had only to meet with his bishop to arrange for his replacement at the church, to move out of his church apartment, store or sell his belongings, and decide what he would have to take with him on the voyage.

Gabriel Hugo's planning was of a different sort. He would need to terminate the lease on his shop in Oporto. He would have to sell off his stock of precious jewelry, gems, and mined gold and silver, a process that might take several weeks.

A more difficult decision was choosing the route from Oporto to Paris. Taking a ship to France would require avoiding the Spanish naval blockade of the coast of Portugal. The two friends decided on a route that would begin overland to the north coast of Spain. Then they would board a ship, sail east along the north coast of Spain, and then north along the east coast of France as far as Nantes. From there, they would take a coach to Paris.

They were ready to depart at the end of 1500.

*　　　　*　　　　*

Arrival!

Other than the normal anxieties of travel, they enjoyed their trip. At 4 o'clock in the afternoon of February 5, 1501, they arrived outside Flamel's house at 51 Rue de Montmorency in Paris. It was down a winding, cobblestone road. Gabriel sighed, smiled and said, "Ah, yes. I remember this house. It has a rather unusual history. Flamel lived in this house with his beloved wife Perenelle, a wealthy Parisian noblewoman."

Father Rodrigo smiled. "I recall the story of your apprenticeship with Flamel. You were 10 years old when he completed the modifications to his spherical astrolabe."

"Yes. I remember well the date—March 21, 1418. Eighty-three years ago! My master told me he was ready to set off on a voyage to the future 'to learn a way to protect our beautiful Earth from a fate I have witnessed in my nightmares.' I helped him hoist a backpack onto his back. Then he placed his hands on the astrolabe and simply disappeared right before my eyes."

"I wonder what happened to that astrolabe. I am astonished that my master is still alive, for that matter. He could be well over 110 years old by now. I am 93 years old, and my poor legs complain every day! I suspect my longevity is due to Flamel's astrolabe."

The priest said, "Well, Flamel's astrolabe was not the same astrolabe you and I and the three Malian sisters modified many years later. That one came from my parishioner Horacio Fuente in Mogadishu. He told me he had used it to travel to the past from the distant future, from a place called Hawaii. He and a group of fellow professors each had acquired spherical astrolabes and modified them according to the detailed instructions contained in a mysterious book found in a steamer trunk in a mansion one of the professors had purchased. The professors used them to travel to the past, our time, to Mogadishu.

"Fuente told me that he had become stranded in the past when a wire broke inside his astrolabe. He spent the rest of his life in that wonderful city, became a member of my congregation, married a wonderful woman, and had a daughter they named Alessandra. Many years later, after Fuente passed away, Alessandra presented the astrolabe to the Portuguese mariner Vasco da Gama, whose fleet of ships had dropped anchor off the coast of Mogadishu.

"Da Gama accepted the astrolabe because he knew it would help him navigate back to Portugal from India. Apparently, that westward voyage was much more treacherous because of the contrary currents off the Cape of Good Hope on the southern tip of the African continent. When I asked da Gama to take me with him on the voyage so that I could return to my home in Oporto, he agreed. Then he returned that astrolabe to me when we arrived in Portugal. As you know, that was the astrolabe we used to alter the course of history." Father Rodrigo paused, then continued. "I wonder whether Flamel still has his astrolabe and what he has been up to since he disappeared."

Gabriel smiled. "I suppose we shall soon find out." He walked up to the entrance of the beautiful house and knocked.

*   *   *

A young African man appeared and opened the door. He smiled at them and bid them set down their bags inside the door. He spoke with a heavily accented Arabic accent. "Greetings. I am Hassan ibn Awolu, Monsieur Flamel's friend. Please, gentlemen, follow me to the drawing room. There you may take a seat and await Monsieur Flamel, who will join you shortly."

The two friends were shocked at the sight of an African man in Paris, especially one with an Arabic accent. Even more shocking was the appearance of Nicolas Flamel when he entered the room. Gabriel spoke first. "My master! How could this be? I recognize you, but it would seem that you haven't aged even a year in the past 83 years!"

Flamel chuckled, grasped Gabriel by the shoulders and kissed him on both cheeks. "My dear apprentice! I apologize for leaving you under such sudden circumstances." He turned to Father Rodrigo and said, "Ah, the good priest I have heard so much about. Your servants did their assigned tasks admirably. We now live in a different and much better world than it was before those beautiful Malian sisters arrived in West Africa."

Neither the priest nor the jeweler could speak. Gabriel Hugo, in particular, had apparently lost the ability to speak. His thoughts were a jumble of confusion: Am I dreaming?? This man cannot be my master!

Father Rodrigo spoke first. "Monsieur Flamel, it is a great pleasure to finally meet the man who created that wonderful device, a device that enabled my servants to travel back in time and prevent the diabolical institution of slavery from traveling to the New World from West Africa!"

"Well, thank you for that compliment. But I assure you it was not I who came up with that plan. It was you! And by the way, I should tell you that your servants Khadija, Sofia and Maryam, carried out your plan perfectly. Now their legacy lives on all around the western hemisphere. And Sofia's grandson Hassan has become an accomplished mariner. It was he who piloted the craft that took us here, and who is staying here in Paris for the time being."

At that point, Gabriel regained the ability to speak. "Monsieur Flamel, please explain how you have not aged."

Flamel's expression turned serious. "The spherical astrolabe is the culprit, I believe." Then he reached into his sweater and pulled out a beautiful amulet. "This amulet absorbed some of the energy of the astrolabe. It originally belonged to a ninth-century caliph, Haroun al-Rashid of Palestine. It was subsequently acquired in the year 1,000 by the emperor Charlemagne, and I acquired it from him. I won't bore you with the details of how I acquired it from him!"

Hugo said, "Well, you must have used your spherical astrolabe to go back in time, isn't that correct?"

"Yes, that's correct. I traveled not only to the past but to the future as well. But after I began wearing the amulet while traveling through time with the astrolabe, the amulet must have absorbed the power of the astrolabe. You see the jewel in the middle? And the fine hair that appears embedded in the jewel? It is said to be a hair from the Virgin Mary. Perhaps that was the source of the amulet's power. The amulet itself eventually became the source of the power to travel through time. It also has stopped me from aging. I found it no longer necessary to use the astrolabe, and left it here.

"Alas, the amulet's power waned and eventually it disappeared. The amulet is no longer a time machine unless used in combination with the astrolabe. However, as I said, the amulet has one other, very important, power. As long as I wear it, the aging process is kept at bay. Despite my appearance, I am over 160 years old."

The two friends were stunned into silence for a few moments. Then it was Father Rodrigo's turn to question Flamel. "So, do you know whatever happened to my parishioner Horacio Fuente's astrolabe? It was his that Gabriel and I modified, the one that the sisters used to travel back to Mali in the year 1446."

"I believe Fuente's astrolabe is in Niumi, along with a large, leather-bound book bearing the title "Um Tempo Longe do Tempo." I collaborated on that book with the eldest of the three sisters, Khadijah. She was Hassan's great aunt, sister of his grandmother Sofia. The plan was to present the book to Khadijah's grand niece Aliyah. It is written in Portuguese and tells the complete story of how our alternate history came into being. Khadijah told me she had planned to store Fuente's astrolabe in her home in Niumi.

"As for my own astrolabe, it is safely stored here in my home. I have a plan for it once all our other plans have been completed." As he said that he smiled at the priest and said, "You, Father, are instrumental in that plan, but just be patient. I will let you know when the time comes!" Father Rodrigo raised his eyebrows but didn't respond.

At that point, Hassan arose and said, "Nicolas, honored guests, may I suggest we move to the dining room? Our noble cook, François, has prepared the evening meal."

* * *

During the meal, there was much conversation about Hugo and Rodrigo's journey from Portugal to Paris. And that conversation naturally led to their questions about how Flamel and Hassan arrived in Paris from Niumi, which Hassan explained was the capital of the newly created Federation of nations on both sides of the Great Ocean. The original name, in Portuguese, of the Federation was the "Mali-Atlantico Federação".

Flamel said, "It was a long trip, very long. And at times perilous. Not so much because of the normal risks of ocean travel, but because of the intermittent warfare between France, Spain and England."

Rodrigo interjected, "And Portugal as well? As we departed from Portugal to begin our journey here, we had some concern that we would be attacked by hostile ships."

Flamel said, "No, Hassan and I didn't need to worry about that particular conflict. Our ship was one of those caravels belonging to the Federation. It was well-armed, of course, but our course kept us well away from the coasts of Portugal, Spain and France. It was only when we began our approach to the Channel between France and England that we worried about an attack from either country.

"But at that point, France was engaged in a war in Italy, and England was at peace, for the moment. As a result, we were not attacked. Our ship docked at the Port of Honfleur, and Hassan and I traveled to Paris by coach. We arrived not long ago. The other 10 sailors aboard our ship have stayed behind at the Port and are enjoying the French coast."

After a moment, François came into the dining room and said with a smile, "Might I suggest you proceed to the salon in the back overlooking the garden? I have prepared a dessert that I think would be better enjoyed in the company of the lovely flowers our caretaker has planted. I have also prepared that wonderful concoction brought to us by our Arab friends, something they call qahwa." The suggestion was welcomed, and the friends moved to the salon.

*　　　　*　　　　*

Gabriel was the first to speak after the group had finished their dessert and qahwa. "Monsieur Flamel, your letter indicated you had a specific purpose in asking us to join you here in Paris. What do you have in mind?"

"Well, before we discuss my plans, allow me to show you around the house and grounds." The group arose and followed Flamel as he walked to the staircase and went up to the upper rooms. There was a bedroom on each side of the hall, a library at the end of the hall, and another set of stairs leading down at the end of the hall. Once Flamel had led them back downstairs to the salon, he motioned for Hassan to open the rear door to the garden. "I apologize for the poor condition of my garden. I have been away too long, and I'm afraid I didn't think to ask my caretaker to undertake gardening duties as well." Rather than taking the group outside in the chilly evening, Flamel turned around and motioned for everyone to take a seat.

Flamel said, "You asked about my plans for you." He paused before continuing. "My purpose has to do with the English exploratory expedition to the New World commissioned by King Henry the Seventh."

This comment took the two friends' breath away. Rodrigo was the first to speak. "Monsieur Flamel, please enlighten us. We had not heard of such an expedition."

Flamel said, "Let me tell you what I learned last year before I decided to embark on this journey to France." He paused for a few moments before continuing. "On one of my trips to the future before my amulet lost its 'charm,' so to speak, I learned of some important events in English history, what I would call 'parallel history.' Here is one event I am sure will interest you—the present English monarch, King Henry the Seventh, would die of consumption on April 21, 1509. His successor would be his second-oldest son, Henry."

Again, Flamel's companions were stunned into silence. Flamel continued, "According to the history I studied, Henry's reign as Henry the Eighth ushered in a disastrous period, a cataclysm in fact."

Father Rodrigo was the first to react. "I have two questions. First, why wouldn't Prince Arthur become king, since he was the older brother? Second, why was his younger brother's reign disastrous?"

Flamel said, "Your first question is the most urgent, and the answer to it will render the second question moot. In the history that I studied in my voyage to the future, I learned that soon after Prince Arthur's marriage to Princess Catherine of Spain, he contracted what the doctors called a 'sweating sickness' that killed him but spared Catherine. The date of his death in that alternate future was the second of April 1502. King Henry was then obliged to name the younger brother, Prince Henry, as his successor. As I mentioned, that younger brother became Henry the Eighth and his reign became a disaster for the entire world. We cannot allow that future to come to pass."

Father Rodrigo asked, "But what could anyone possibly do to prevent Prince Arthur from contracting that deadly disease? We— Hugo and I—have never even met any members of the English aristocracy."

Flamel smiled again. Then, arising from the table, he gestured to the doorway leading into another room. "Let us go into my laboratory, and I will explain my plan to you." The four of them— Nicolas, Gabriel, Father Rodrigo and Hassan—walked out of the room and into the laboratory.

Flamel turned to the others after everyone had entered the laboratory. He said, "Before I explain what you see here, let me answer the second part of your question, Father Rodrigo. Although none of us has ever met the prince, a man who has met him is on his way here from his aborted voyage to the New World. His name is Captain John Cabot. He was commissioned by King Henry to explore the New World in the hope of establishing trade relations with the rulers of China.

"However, the reason Captain Cabot abandoned his mission is twofold. First, he learned that the land of China lies far beyond the western side of the continent he and the other explorers have called the New World. And second, he learned that he alone would be able to arrange our introduction to the prince and his new bride."

Father Rodrigo said, "It sounds like you're saying that Captain Cabot already knew the prince. Is that right?"

"Yes, that is correct. He met the prince when the prince was a young adolescent. In fact, the prince is still very young, as is Princess Catherine."

Gabriel looked about the room, momentarily distracted by what looked like a jeweler's shop. Then he turned to Flamel and said, "So, I'm guessing that Cabot's familiarity with the young prince will enable him to obtain an invitation to the wedding. Is that what you're suggesting? But why would Cabot be interested in asking that we— Father Rodrigo and myself—be allowed to attend the wedding?"

"Ah, now we get to the reason we are standing in my laboratory. Maybe you noticed a tray of small gold bands, and a small jar of gemstones on the counter." He turned to Hassan and said, "Would you be so kind as to explain to our guests the nature of the gemstones and where you found them?"

Hassan walked to the counter and removed several of the stones from the jar. He held them out and said, "These are emerald-green chrome tourmalines. Although they're rare, I found these in my home country of Quonambec, southwest across the Atlantic Ocean. A traditional healer there sold me 20 tourmalines, each approximately seven millimeters in diameter. Emerald-green tourmalines have magnetic properties capable of 'untangling'—to use an interesting word—roadblocks in the body's energy passages." He handed two stones to Gabriel and two to Rodrigo, who examined them closely before handing them back. Hassan kept the remaining 18 tourmalines in his hand.

Gabriel turned to Flamel and asked, "Monsieur Flamel, what do you plan on doing with the stones?"

Flamel chuckled. "What I will do is hand all of them to you. I will ask you to set one stone in each of 20 gold rings, which you will design and make. My little laboratory is equipped with gold solder, jeweler's torches and other tools and materials."

Father Rodrigo smiled. "Ah, I understand your plan. But I am confused. Two of the rings will be presented to Prince Arthur and Princess Catherine on the occasion of their wedding in England. You are counting on the rings to counteract the disease." Father Rodrigo paused and continued, "How that would come about, I don't understand. Nor do I understand how you would know their ring size.

"But what I also don't understand is why you ask Hugo to make 18 additional rings. Who would those rings be for?"

Flamel said, "First, let us go to the work bench and I will answer those questions." The group walked to the bench and Flamel resumed, "The properties of the tourmalines, as I said, include assisting the body's energy flow, through an inherent magnetic property of the stones. That property is well known among indigenous peoples all over the world.

"The illness that Prince Arthur and Princess Catherine would contract—unless prevented by these stones—is similar to a disease common in tropical regions. The indigenous peoples of those regions often wore jewelry made from these stones to combat the fevers and sickness caused by the disease. Others persons who might also contract the disease would be King Henry's youngest daughter, Princess Mary, his other son, Prince Henry Junior, their spouses when they eventually marry, and other people who will receive the rings as gifts."

Gabriel asked, "But how would such a disease occur in a region like England? Surely the disease you speak of is one only found in the tropics."

Flamel shook his head. "You may have forgotten that England has had trading relationships with countries in the tropics. It is likely that the diseases traveled to England along with the animals and trade goods obtained in the tropics."

Gabriel said, "And my second question: their ring size? How will I make rings of the correct size?"

"The two rings for Henry Junior and his eventual betrothed will be sized for a child's hand. You only need to approximate their sizes. A jeweler can adjust them later as necessary. And the other rings' sizes can be altered later as necessary."

Gabriel asked one more question, "You spoke of Mary's and Henry Junior's spouses 'when they eventually marry.' Do you know something we don't know?" When Gabriel asked this, he smiled knowingly.

"Of course, I know something you don't know! You should have no doubt by now. Those two will marry, without a doubt. I am working on my plan as we speak."

*   *   *

At the workbench

Gabriel had enjoyed himself at the jeweler's bench during the past two hours. Finally, satisfied with his work, he held the soldering iron in one hand and a completed ring in the other. He said to Flamel, "What do you think? I have set a stone in this band. It's firmly bonded to the gold band with the gold solder." He held out the ring to Flamel, who took it and examined it closely.

"It looks beautiful!" Handing it back he said, "I'm sure the other rings will be just as beautiful."

Gabriel turned back to the workbench and resumed his work. Hassan said, "Perhaps, gentlemen, we should go out in the garden and wait for Monsieur Hugo to join us there with the rings. Once we are satisfied with their beauty, we have only to await the arrival of Captain Cabot."

Father Rodrigo said, "I'm looking forward to exploring Paris again. It has been many years. And I have never explored the Marais District! How soon do you expect Cabot to arrive?"

"Captain Cabot's ships should arrive by mid-July."

CHAPTER TWELVE

July 21, 1501

During the 28-day voyage across the Great Ocean, Cabot's crews on the two ships had been hard at work on the dangerous ocean. Mattea and John's sons worked as hard as Sebastian, Arne, Shay, Balder and Aponi. The work was difficult, but Cabot and his crew were excellent mariners.

But now, Mattea's excitement grew as she caught sight of the coast of France and the entrance to the English Channel. She and everyone else were tired being on board a crowded ship on the high seas.

John walked up to Mattea and said, "According to what Janaina told me, we will be in the Port of Honfleur soon. From there, we will send word to Monsieur Flamel, who will arrange for carriages to transport all of us to his home. There, we will enjoy a few months of rest and excitement in the city of Paris as the esteemed Master Alchemist regales us with his tales of the past and future!"

*　　　*　　　*

Paris and Bristol

During the month that Cabot's crews explored Paris, Aponi was fascinated by the French city on the Seine. But she was even more intrigued by Captain Cabot's description of the English city of Bristol and the royal family. Especially "Crown Prince" Arthur. She didn't know why she had become so fascinated by the concept of royalty. She couldn't wait to see the prince, his father King Henry, and the royal grounds in the city of Bristol.

She was a little curious about how the English would view her, so she approached Mattea for her advice. "How do you think they will react to seeing me among the crew? I do not think they will be surprised to see Balder, since he is a Norseman like several others of the crew. But how would the English react to a woman of the Onondaga Nation?"

Mattea said, "I have no doubt they will be intrigued. I don't think the English have ever seen one of your people, although they no doubt have heard tales told by the Norse explorers."

"What are the members of the English royalty like? And Bristol?"

Mattea smiled. "Bristol is a fascinating city, very modern with a large port, shops and homes. John and I lived there for a time as we waited for the king to grant our request for an expedition to China. After John returned from the first exploratory voyage, the king granted his request for another expedition of longer duration. The king agreed to an expedition farther north than the one undertaken by Colombo. Of course, as we learned, the land we encountered was not China, which lies beyond the western shore of what is called the New World.

"Now our hope is to meet with the king at the Royal Maritime House in Bristol. And I'm sure the English royal family will be very pleasant. Their civilization is very high, rich and sometimes ostentatious. The prince and his betrothed, Princess Catherine of Aragon, are very young. They are inexperienced but no doubt very educated."

"Where is Aragon? It doesn't sound like an English city."

"The princess comes from a royal family in Spain; the wedding was arranged to improve relations between England and Spain.

"But don't worry about anything. Captain Cabot will arrange the meetings and explain our purpose. Once he, Father Rodrigo and the jeweler Gabriel Hugo meet with the royal family, everything will no doubt proceed smoothly."

Aponi sighed and pushed her desire a bit further to the front. "I would dearly love to meet the royal couple; even the king! I used to dream that I would one day meet a royal person. But in my dreams, the royal person was not of my people; indeed, my people didn't have royalty, at least not like the figures in my dreams. I know that the Norse have royalty but I never met any of them."

Mattea thought for a moment and then said, "Well, I think the king and royal family would enjoy meeting you. In all likelihood, they would be fascinated by the idea of meeting someone from across the Atlantic Ocean, especially someone from the Onondaga Nation. I will ask John what he thinks."

*   *   *

Bristol

Cabot's two ships and crews—15 sailors plus Sebastian, Aponi and Balder on La Cristianne, and 18 sailors plus Captain Cabot, Madame Jacobella, their two younger sons, Father Rodrigo and Gabriel Hugo on Le Michel—got underway just after dawn on October thirty-first. The seven-day voyage was blessed with calm waters and fair weather, despite the lateness of the year. The two ships docked at Bristol Harbor just after noon on November the eighth.

Cabot was surprised to see what looked like an official greeting party awaiting them. He turned to Mattea and said, "It looks like Monsieur Flamel has arranged a reception for us!"

After the crews disembarked and assembled just beyond the dock, Cabot saw Prince Arthur and two attendants come walking toward the group. The prince smiled and reached out to take Cabot's hands. "Welcome, my friend." Turning to Mattea, he said, "And welcome to you as well, Lady Jacobella. I am eager to learn the results of your voyage, about which I have heard very little. Nor has word reached the king or the others. They and my betrothed, Princess Catherine of Aragon, await us at the royal residence nearby. When you are ready, I will escort you there."

Cabot bowed and thanked the prince. "My Lord, the crew on our two ships number 36 sailors and two guests from the New World. Will there be sufficient accommodation for them?"

Prince Arthur smiled and looked surprised. "Certainly, there will be ample accommodation at our Maritime House. I am sure my father, especially, will look forward to speaking with your guests from the New World and learning more about their people! Come, let us move away from the windy docks and find some shelter."

*   *   *

The plan moves forward

Mattea was relieved to see the quality of accommodations prepared for them. There were three comfortable rooms in a small stone house, one for Mattea and Captain Cabot and one each for Aponi and Balder. There was a large dormitory building where the sailors, including the Cabot sons, would sleep. "John, I think this is excellent! King Henry no doubt is expressing his gratitude for our successful return." She paused for a moment and added, "I just hope he isn't too disappointed when he learns that we didn't reach China."

"Yes, our report must be tailored to emphasize what we did discover, especially the size of the New World. Of course, he will be very interested to learn the fate of Cristoforo Colombo. Our discovery of the `Kaniataro Wanenneh'—the `Big Waterway' in the Mohawk language—will fascinate him. Perhaps most interesting of all will be the report of our encounter with the three leaders of the 'Haudenosaunee Confederacy'—Tekahawi'ta, Ayenwatha and Jikonhassee."

Mattea looked concerned. "I do worry a little about the king's reaction when we report on our discovery of the nation of Guanahani."

"What do you mean?" How could a little group of islands be a cause of worry to the leader of the strongest nation in Europe?"

"Well, John, you are forgetting our discussions with Captain Janaina Watu concerning the Malian federation, stretching southwards from Guanahani to the land of Quonambec and most of the western hemisphere. How do you think the king will react to that?"

Cabot was silent for a few moments before responding. "I have to admit to a bit of uncertainty about the king's reaction to news of an empire across the Atlantic, especially one that originates in Mali, Africa. Do you think he would be alarmed to think there might be a powerful empire that could challenge England's might?"

Mattea paused, but then said, "I think if we emphasized how successful the Malians have been in curbing the power of Spain and Portugal, King Henry would perhaps relax a bit. After all, Henry himself has been very active in keeping those kingdoms from dominating Europe and indeed the entire world."

*   *   *

For the rest of that afternoon, the sailors were busy settling into their accommodations. A few of them joined Aponi, Balder, Sebastian and his brothers in a stroll around what Arthur had called the little royal "village" abutting the seaport. Aponi tried not to be too distracted by all the attention shown to her by the curious residents. She understood their reactions to her—a very tall young woman with reddish-brown skin, long black hair, and jet-black eyes. Several times, elderly women approached her and extended their hands to hers. Aponi smiled and spoke a few words in the limited English she had learned from Mattea and John. The reaction from the women was that of gleeful surprise.

After Aponi and the little group had been walking for about an hour, they returned to their rooms.

*   *   *

Making plans

The staff at the Maritime House prepared an early dinner for the crews. During the meal a representative of the prince arrived to let them know of the plan for the next day. "His Majesty has returned from his meetings in London, and will meet with you during the midday meal tomorrow. He is looking forward to a full report of your expedition."

After the announcement, Captain Cabot informed his crews that he was calling a general meeting that very evening. "It will be short, but important. Please bring any questions and suggestions you may have."

The crews were summoned back to the Maritime House two hours later. Cabot explained what he thought the agenda for the king's meeting would be the next day. "I expect the first order of business will be introductions of our crew and guests. Then Mattea and I will present our report of the expedition. We don't know what the king's reaction will be, other than disappointment that we did not reach the land of China. But he will be very interested to learn of the vast continent that lies on the western shores of the Atlantic Ocean. We will describe our meeting with the leaders of the Haudenosaunee Confederacy. At that point, rather than moving on to a report concerning the Malian confederacy, I believe Mattea will introduce Aponi and Balder."

There were several moments of silence before Shay Black stood and commented. "Captain, sooner or later, the king must be informed of the existence of the new civilization that the Malians have created. Surely you can convince him of the potential for alliances between England and Mali."

Mattea turned to her husband and said, "I agree with Shay, John. As we discussed earlier, I believe the king must learn of the Malians and the nature of the civilization across the Atlantic. That civilization is not warlike in the least and its people have no interest in becoming an empire. We should stress the primary focus of the Malians, which is to raise the level of health and prosperity in the New World. The Malians are also working to thwart the efforts of Portugal and Spain to exploit the New World with slave labor from Africa."

Cabot nodded. "Yes, you have convinced me. I think, Mattea, you should be the one who describes that civilization and in particular what we found in the land of Guanahani."

At that point there were a few moments of silence. Then Father Rodrigo rose and spoke. "Captain, on another subject, as you know, my friend and colleague, the Parisian jeweler, Gabriel Hugo, is with us." Turning to Hugo and smiling, Rodrigo continued, "He is perhaps too shy or hesitant to bring up the topic of the two masterpieces he has created for the royal couple." Again, the priest smiled at the jeweler before continuing. "The two masterpieces are beautiful engagement rings for the prince and princess. Our hope is to ask the king to allow us to present the rings to the couple at some point before the ceremony. What point do you think that should be?"

Cabot said, "We will have to see how our meeting with the king is proceeding. I will look for an opportunity to bring up the subject."

CHAPTER THIRTEEN

King Henry's dream

Henry's London meetings with the nobles and townspeople were tiresome. They were always tiresome. So many disputes, so much greed and suspicion. But the worst part of this most recent series of meetings was the insufferable arrogance of the priests. My God, please spare me any further interference from these fools! Henry had always tried to keep the clergy at arm's distance. He acknowledged their right to a certain portion of the royal income from rents and taxes, but had always chafed at the ignorance and prejudices of the priesthood. Especially their attitude toward the Jews. Where those bigots get their beliefs, I'll never know. `Christ killers' is their constant refrain. They speak such calumnies in their churches, to their colleagues, to the local nobles—surely it is a poison! They point to the Holy Bible, to the passages in which—in their view—it was the desire of the Jewish people in Israel to do away with Our Lord. Such ignorance! It was the Romans who killed Our Lord, not the Jews!

Despite Henry's strong conviction with regard to the errors of the clergy, he had not, before now, felt strong enough to challenge the clergy. Especially after the dreadful war with the malcontent Warbeck.

Perhaps it was the level of bile arising in his gut that day, but his sleep that night left him with a new feeling of strength. He wasn't sure when he awoke the next morning what exactly had convinced him that he must no longer fear the clergy. It might have been his dreams, in which he felt an overwhelming resolve that he must do something to curb the power of the priests. Not the Church itself; no, rather, the fools who think of themselves as a power apart from the Monarchy. They do not get their arrogance from Rome; they get it from the avaricious landowners who seek to bar talented foreigners from entering our land!

As Henry ate breakfast in his rooms at the London palace, he brought his thoughts back to the present. A level of excitement began to emerge as he recalled the briefing given to him two days before. The Cabot ships had returned from the New World. But not much more information than that, except there was a report of a native of the New World aboard Cabot's ships; or was it two natives? A woman and a man. A very tall, beautiful young woman.

With that thought of speaking with this exotic stranger in the forefront of his thoughts, Henry arose from his table and called for his coach to take him to Bristol.

*   *   *

A surprising afternoon

"Captain Cabot, Madame Jacobella, you are requested to assemble your crew and guests and proceed to the Maritime House for the midday meal. You will be the guests of King Henry." The young woman who delivered that request had identified herself as the daughter of one of Henry's nobles, a friend of the prince himself.

It wasn't difficult to rouse the crew and guests, as they had been awake and outside for a few hours already. Mattea caught Sebastian's eye and directed him to spread the word that everyone must report to the Maritime House an hour before noon.

As the crews and guests entered the great hall of the Maritime House, they were hailed as "the discoverers of the New World." Prince Arthur and his betrothed Princess Catherine stood nearby and greeted them warmly. Arthur said, "Come, Captain Cabot and Madame Jacobella, you shall sit at my father's table. Your crew will sit at the two long tables on the sides. And the King has asked that the guests from the New World and Paris sit at his table as well."

Mattea directed the sailors to the seats set aside for them. Cabot said to Aponi, Balder, Father Rodrigo and Gabriel Hugo, "Follow me, it seems you will be honored guests at the King's table." Cabot paused and said to Aponi and Balder, "But be careful. The King is a crafty ruler, a master of gathering information. Especially information that he thinks you might be inclined to withhold. So, whenever possible, allow me and Mattea to give our report without any commentary from yourselves. If the King asks you a direct question, of course answer it truthfully; but skillfully. Most likely he will be content with information about your homeland, how you came to be our guests, and such matters. Avoid saying anything about the Malians. That will be a delicate subject better brought up in the context of the report I and my lady give."

Mattea was surprised to see that there were ten seats at the King's table. Prince Arthur indicated that Balder and Aponi would sit together in the seats on the left side of the table. Next to them, to their right, would sit Rodrigo and Hugo. John's seat would be to their right. Mattea's seat would be to the right of John's. The prince and princess would sit in the two seats at the other end of the table. The seat in the very middle of the table was set aside for the King. That left one seat undesignated. But who would sit next to him?

Once everyone had taken their seats, King Henry entered the pavilion. A murmur arose when the Bishop of Bristol walked in immediately after the King. Henry walked to the seat in the middle of the table, turned to the bishop and gestured to the seat next to his. Then Henry smiled at Mattea, John, and the rest of the guests before he spoke. "Honored guests, family and friends. The expedition to the New World has successfully returned. We are all eager to receive the report of Captain Cabot. But first, I acknowledge another guest, the Honorable Bishop Leopold of Bristol.

"But before we ask Captain Cabot and Lady Jacobella to present their report, I believe we should take our midday meal, as I am very hungry!" Henry turned to the two servants standing at the entrance to the kitchen and gestured for them to begin serving the meal to the guests.

The first to be served, of course, were the King and the others at his table. John and Mattea were relieved to be given a respite before having to commence their presentation. But that respite did not last long. The first person the King spoke to once the food had been set on the table was Mattea, but very quietly. "My Lady Jacobella," the King said in a low voice. "I want to reassure you that you have no cause for worry concerning that most delicate subject we discussed before you set out on the expedition." Then he winked, smiled, and spoke in an even lower voice, almost a whisper, "My friend the bishop is in for a bit of a surprise, I'm afraid. But no matter; he will learn that being a bishop in my realm is full of surprises. Watch how his expression changes as the day progresses!"

More surprises

Mattea was careful to avoid the gaze of Bishop Leopold during the meal. In fact, it seemed the bishop only had Prince Arthur to talk to, and only sporadically at that, since Arthur was much more interested in talking to his betrothed.

Finally, the King arose and addressed the guests. "Honorable Bishop Leopold, Prince Arthur, Princess Catherine, we are honored today by the return of Captain Cabot, his wife Lady Mattea Jacobella, and the crews and guests on their expedition to the New World." He paused to allow the murmurs to subside. Then he said, "Captain Cabot will begin the report of the expedition."

Cabot stood, bowed to the King and the Bishop, and took a deep breath. "My Lord, you asked for a complete report and you shall have it. First, let me state right off that we did not reach the land of China. We learned that China is a continent far to the west of the continent we found."

Henry signaled for Cabot to pause. "Captain, how did you learn the location of China if you did not go there?"

This was the question Cabot was afraid of. But Mattea was right— the King was entitled to learn the truth without delay. "Your Majesty, our expedition encountered people every time we made landfall. First, we met the Beothuk people who live on an island west and south of Iceland. We helped them defend themselves against persistent attacks by the Mikmak people who inhabit a larger group of islands north of Beothuk Island. When we inquired about China, the Beothuk people knew nothing of China. However, it was on that island where we met a most remarkable young woman and a Norseman, both of whom asked to accompany us for the remainder of our journey. Those two people are sitting at this table, and you will soon hear from them directly. But let me continue before they tell you more about their land.

"After leaving the Beothuk land, we sailed farther west and encountered a most exotic civilization on what we learned was the eastern shore of a vast continent. It was there that we learned that China was a distant land far to the west of that continent.

"Finally, the last land we encountered was where we learned the most amazing fact of all. I will ask my wife, Mattea Jacobella, to tell you about that discovery."

Mattea smiled at her husband, then rose and acknowledged the King and the Bishop. Then she spoke. "My Lord, honored guests. My husband spoke of the many inhabited lands we visited and the varied people we met. Indeed, on two occasions we helped groups of people defend themselves against hostile aggressive neighbors, by building walls and other fortifications. We taught them how to improve their watercraft in order to travel farther and faster on the open ocean.

"But it was on the last island nation we visited, a land the people have named Guanahani, where we encountered the most astounding sight of all—Africans, Spanish, English, Arawak and Taino people, all living and working together peacefully to improve their lives.

"One of those people, a very impressive woman named Janaina Watu, was captain of a caravel at anchor in their harbor. Captain Watu told us the people there were citizens of a seagoing organization they called the Malian-Quonambec Federation. The Federation was created jointly by people from Mali and the New World, more specifically, the peoples of Mali, Africa, and Quonambec, the southern continent directly across the Great Ocean from Africa."

At this point, King Henry once again interrupted the report to ask for clarification. "Madame Jacobella, your account is almost beyond comprehension—Africans in the New World? Europeans as well? And most remarkable of all—or should I say, the most alarming of all—is that Federation." The king paused as if searching for words, then resumed. "You say this Federation was solely concerned with a charitable purpose. How can you be sure there was no other purpose, for example, a military or imperialistic purpose?"

Mattea sighed, then answered. "Well, Your Highness, there was indeed what we should acknowledge as a military purpose. Captain Janaina Watu wore a military uniform with insignia of the federation. Moreover, in our discussions with her about the nature of the Federation, she told us of its origins—to block the expansion of the Portuguese slave trade into the New World. In fact, the Federation was created by Malians who had formerly been enslaved by the Portuguese. The Malians created a fleet of some 40 caravels—some taken from Portuguese slavers, some built by the Malians using the Portuguese caravels as models—with which to patrol the waters of the Atlantic Ocean and seize ships involved in the expansion of slavery to the New World."

Henry was silent for a moment, then asked, "So, this Janaina woman... She was an African? From Mali?"

"No, Your Highness. She was a Taino woman from Quonambec. She was tall, olive-complexioned, with straight black hair, and quite beautiful. She commanded a caravel of some 15 men and women that was stationed in the little nation of Guanahani. But some of her sailors were African, or mixed African-Taino, or European. In fact, the first two of her sailors we encountered were Spaniards. They assisted us in entering their well-concealed harbor."

"Spaniards? How did Spaniards ever get to the New World?? He paused then added, "Ah... perhaps from Admiral Colombo's expedition?"

Mattea smiled. "Yes, I suppose that might be possible. Admiral Colombo himself was reportedly in the region; settled there, in fact."

"What! Colombo? He had been reported lost at sea years ago. Now you say he settled in this... Guanahani? How so?"

"Your Highness, I do not know how Colombo ended up in Guanahani."

Henry seemed at a loss for words for several minutes. Mattea decided to take advantage of the king's silence to proceed with her report. "Your Highness, as was mentioned by my husband, we have as guests in our crew, a young woman named Aponi and a man named Balder, sitting at our table. Would you like to hear their accounts?"

Henry was brought back to the present at the mention of the guests from the New World. "Certainly, if they wish to tell us about themselves, I would love to hear their story."

Balder stood first. "Your Highness, I lived all my adult life among the Beothuk people, but I am not Beothuk. I am Norse. I asked to join Captain Cabot's expedition when he and his crew helped the Beothuk improve their defenses. Perhaps I still have some of my

Norse people's love of exploration. But a much more interesting story will come from my young friend here, Aponi." He nodded at Aponi and sat down.

Aponi stood, smiled at Balder, and thanked the king for hosting this gathering. "Your Highness, like Balder, I am not a native Beothuk. We both grew into adulthood there, but from very different backgrounds. He is Norse. I am Onondaga. My people are native to the New World. I was a young member of an Onondaga exploratory mission in the ocean around Beothuk Island when my boat was attacked by Mikmak sailors. I was the only survivor. I was rescued by Beothuk people and later adopted by a Beothuk family. Like Balder, I suppose I decided to join Captain Cabot's expedition out of a sense of adventure."

The king waited for Aponi to pause and then spoke. "Aponi, you say you are native to the New World, Onondaga, I believe. Were you from that land that Captain Cabot called an `exotic civilization?'"

"No, Your Highness. But from a land neighboring that civilization. There are many communities of native peoples in that continent. The one that Captain Cabot referred to was led by three individuals—a woman named `Jikonhassee,' a man named `Ayenwatha,' and a most remarkable man called `Tekahawi'ta.'"

"Why `remarkable,' this Tekahawi'ta?"

"Well, Your Highness, for one thing he seemed to be some sort of holy man, or seer, or prophet. The others viewed him with great reverence. And when the others said they hadn't heard of a land called China, this Tekahawi'ta knew of it. It was he who told us where the land of China lay. He also told us that as we sailed farther south, we would encounter another civilization."

"And that civilization was the one led by this woman named Janaina Watu?"

"Well, Your Highness, she was not the leader, merely a naval captain of some sort. The country of Guanahani, where we met Janaina, was merely a part of a larger federation called Quonambec.

Janaina described the federation's purpose as protecting the peoples and lands of the New World from exploitation and enslavement by the Spanish."

"Ah, once again a reference to the Spanish. But I am confused. It has been reported thus far that there were Spanish people among the peoples of the New World, including Admiral Cristoforo Colombo, who was thought to be lost at sea. If the Spanish were thought to be enemies of the New World, how is that some of them are helping to build up the New World?"

"I did not hear many details of how the Spaniards ended up working with Janaina's people. But the Spaniards we encountered there certainly did not seem to be unhappy. They seemed to be very enthusiastic members of the Federation."

That comment intrigued Princess Catherine. She said, "Your Highness, I have some questions, with your leave." When the king nodded, she stood and spoke. "Aponi, Lady Jacobella and Captain Cabot, I presume you are aware of the history of hostilities between Spain and Portugal in the recent past. Have you come to any conclusions as to the reasons for those hostilities? My family, and all the royals and people of Spain, are deeply concerned by those hostilities, in particular the reason for them. As far as anyone can discern, Portugal and Spain had not been enemies before the hostilities began. To what do you attribute those hostilities? They have created much hardship, and both countries have suffered tremendous economic losses, especially to our shipping industries. "

Captain Cabot answered. "We heard nothing of the hostilities you referred to. Nor did we witness any attacks during our journey here. Perhaps Father Rodrigo can answer your question, since he is a native of Portugal."

Father Rodrigo frowned, but stood to reply to the princess's question. "I believe the hostilities between the two countries were related to Portugal's repeated and pervasive attempts to create an economy based on slavery, in particular the enslavement of Africans.

My theory is that some of Portugal's wealthy shipowners and other members of the mercantile class seized on that idea in order to compete more effectively with Spain.

"As you know, I had spent my entire ministry in East Africa, and only returned to my native Portugal a few years ago. Monsieur Hugo, although a native of Paris, has lived in Oporto since long before I returned. Perhaps he might care to comment on my theory."

Hugo stood and said to the princess, "I believe Father Rodrigo's theory is quite correct. In my profession as a jeweler, I often had occasion to hear my clients and their friends espouse the very ideas you have put forward. These battles were simply the result of Portuguese desire to expand slavery.

"But it has been years since the last battles between the Spanish and Portuguese, more than seven years in fact. I believe they wealthy merchants finally realized that attempting to profit from the slave trade was a hopeless endeavor. So, in my opinion, such attacks are a thing of the past, thanks be to God."

The princess nodded, thanked Father Rodrigo and Hugo, and sat down. Then Father Rodrigo broached the subject that had brought him and his friend to Bristol. "Your Highness, this might be a good time for Monsieur Hugo and myself to make a presentation to Princess Catherine and Prince Arthur." When the king smiled, Rodrigo turned to Hugo and nodded.

Hugo said to the prince and princess, "Your Royal Highnesses, the good Father Rodrigo and I decided last month to present a gift to you on the occasion of your imminent betrothal to one another. The gift is a set of matching rings, one for each of you and one each for Catherine's parents, Queen Isabella and King Ferdinand of unified Spain."

The prince and princess looked at one another. The princess said, "Monsieur Hugo and Father Rodrigo, we would be most honored to accept your gift. If you have brought the rings with you to this gathering, we would love to see them."

Hugo said, "Yes, we did bring the rings in anticipation of your answer." He picked up a small package from the table next to him and handed it to Father Rodrigo. "In light of the holy event we all look forward to, it is fitting that our good priest should present the gift to you both."

The priest walked to the other end of the table and handed the package to Princess Catherine. She eagerly opened it and gasped when she saw the rings inside. She lifted the rings out of the little box and showed them to Prince Arthur. The prince and princess held them up, smiling, and showed them to the king. Arthur said, "Monsieur Hugo, these are truly the most beautiful rings! And the stones—what are they? They catch the light in a most unusual way."

Hugo said, "The stones are emerald-green chrome tourmalines, a very rare gem with unusual properties."

"Unusual? How so?"

Father Rodrigo was afraid of what Hugo might answer, so he answered the question instead. "According to tradition, the stones have a beneficial effect on one's health—fighting off illness and colds, for example. Who knows if the claims are true, of course."

The princess smiled and tried on one of the rings. "Oh, it fits perfectly! Arthur, try on the other one!"

Arthur did so, and his fit perfectly as well. He turned at Catherine, then back at Hugo and the priest. "We thank you both for these most beautiful rings. I think we shall not take them off from this moment on. And I am sure my betrothed's parents will be most honored by your gift."

*   *   *

The rest of the luncheon came to an end shortly after the presentation of the rings when the king announced he had several important appointments scheduled for later that afternoon. But as the guests were starting to leave the room and before the king arose to leave, Hugo approached him and presented him with four of the other rings he had made. "Your Highness, I have made rings similar to the ones I presented to the Prince and Princess. It is my hope that you will present these two rings to your daughter, Mary, and your son, Henry Junior, when they are ready to be married. And the other two to their spouses as well."

Henry smiled and accepted the rings. "Thank you, Monsieur Hugo. I will keep the rings safe until then." Hugo bowed, thanked Henry, and walked back to his table where Father Rodrigo waited. Then the two of them joined the rest of the guests leaving the room.

As Hugo and Father Rodrigo walked back to their apartment, the priest said, "I saw that you managed to present the rings to the king. Well done. We can only hope that he presents the rings to Mary, Henry Junior and their spouses, and that they wear them when the time comes."

Hugo said, "Yes. He accepted them and agreed to my request. I still have the remaining rings in my trunk. They will be presented to their intended recipients as the occasions present themselves." Hugo paused and added, "Well, on another subject. Your reply to the princess's question about the fighting between Portugal and Spain apparently satisfied the princess. Yet, as you know, your answer wasn't a complete answer. One wonders how satisfied the princess really was. Do you think she will press her inquiry further?"

"We can only hope that she won't. She might find my answer satisfactory; yet even if not, her response is of no consequence to you or me."

*   *   *

The interaction between King Henry and Bishop Leopold was, however, quite different. Henry had decided to put an end to—or at the least render impotent—the clergy's insistence on perpetuating the English prejudice against Jews. He wasted no time in acting on his resolve. As the guests were leaving, the king approached the bishop and put his hand on his sleeve. Addressing him by his name instead of his title, he said quietly, "Leo, you and I have a matter to discuss. Let's go to my office." They began walking out of the banquet room.

Leo replied, "Does the matter have anything to do with Lady Jacobella? I am aware of the rumor that she is a Jew. I also heard that you informed her of the long-standing intolerance toward her people here in England."

The king opened the door to his office and gestured for the bishop to enter. Then he said, "It is that long-standing intolerance that I wish to discuss with you. It is my firm belief that it must come to an end. Or, at the very least, that intolerance must not manifest itself towards Lady Jacobella in the least. There will be consequences, Leo, should it come to my attention that you have encouraged or ignored such intolerance. Do you understand me?"

The bishop smirked. "Yes, I understand you. But you perhaps do not fully understand me or my position. I am an officer of the Holy Church. The Church is a protected institution in England. Protected, most especially, from interference by the Crown or its agents."

The king laughed out loud. "You flatter yourself, Leo. I find your attitude offensive and hollow. You have no authority in the civil realm and you know it. Such power you ascribe to the Church in England is nothing more than an appeal to knavery." The king paused, shut the door to his office, and turned back to the bishop. "Let me be blunt, Leo. If I hear a hint that you are spreading, or allowing, anti-Jewish prejudice, I will have you arrested and imprisoned. You may complain to the archbishop, to the Cardinals, to the Pope himself, but it will not get you out of prison. I will make your life miserable, Leo—you can believe it!"

The bishop was stunned into silence. The king continued. "And one more thing, Leo. I am ordering you to convene a local meeting of priests here. I will be present. I will personally convey my feelings on this subject. Do you get my meaning? I have the power to enforce my decisions in civil matters, and prejudice or threats towards others, even when based on religious prejudice, is a civil matter. It will not be tolerated! I will order the arrest and imprisonment of anyone I find who has encouraged or permitted anti-Jewish activity. Do you understand me? Do you wish to find out the extent of my power? You would do well to recall how I came to power. Enough said!" With that, the king opened the door and said, "Good day, Leo. Let me know when you have scheduled the meeting of priests."

* * *

The very next morning was hardly soon enough for King Henry to speak in more depth to Captain Cabot and Madame Jacobella. He sent a messenger to their lodging asking them if he might speak to them privately at his rooms.

Mattea was surprised when the messenger delivered the request. "Well, what do you think he wants to talk about? He already reassured me about the Jewish question. Maybe he wants to know more about the Malian federation. That is probably his concern—that there might be a mighty naval power that could challenge England's."

"Either subject will not be a problem. We should be forthright and frank; he's a perceptive person." They left their room and walked to the king's residence.

A servant met them and escorted them into the king's drawing room. "He will be with you shortly." They stood near the fireplace and waited.

A few minutes later the king entered accompanied by a man neither John nor Mattea had seen before. Henry gestured for them to have a seat. "Thank you both for responding to my request." Gesturing to his companion he said, "This is Professor Arnold Beck from the University of Cambridge. He will be assisting us in our discussion of Mali and what you have called the New World."

Once everyone had taken a seat, the king said, "Professor Beck is what you might call an `Africanist,' an academic expert on the subject of Africa generally. I'll let Professor Beck tell us more about his speciality. We'll also have a chance to ask him about the information we heard yesterday from yourselves and the members of your crew, which I summarized for him last evening." The king nodded to the professor and said, "Proceed, Professor!"

Beck was a large man, overweight, with an imposing air about him. His beard was long and unkempt. He smiled at the king and turned to John and Mattea with a serious expression. He spoke first to John. "Captain Cabot, the king has provided me with something of a summary of the report you and your wife gave yesterday. As the king has said, my academic speciality is the study of African history and its people. Let me ask you about one aspect of the report you provided."

He paused and looked through some papers he had set on the table. "You have provided a most remarkable story, the most remarkable part in my opinion is your description of a native woman who seemed to be a military leader of some kind. Not only a military leader but a commander of a naval craft called a caravel." Again, he paused before continuing. "Would you mind describing the caravel in a little more detail?"

Cabot smiled and answered, "The caravel looked very much like the caravel La Cristianne, one of the two ships provided to us by the king. In fact, it looked like a caravel in every way, as if it had been built here in Bristol Harbor."

Beck raised his eyebrows and asked, "What is your opinion as to where that ship came from?"

"Professor Beck, it was my impression that the ship had been built by the Malians themselves. Captain Janaina talked at some length about the Federation, its origin and purpose. Although I hadn't asked specifically about the ship she commanded, it was my assumption that it was constructed by the Malian Federation. I have no reason to think otherwise."

Professor Beck was silent for a moment before responding. "Now, as the king mentioned, my academic speciality is the history and culture of West Africa in general. One thing that strikes me as unusual, very unusual in fact, is your claim that the ship we're talking about was a caravel. There are no caravels anywhere in West Africa. The ships in use there are small, rudimentary crafts known as `pirogues.' They are propelled by oars, not sails." He paused again and continued. "Captain Cabot, there is absolutely no likelihood that an African craft such as a pirogue could have traveled across the Atlantic Ocean."

Cabot frowned and said, "Perhaps you misheard me, or the report's summary didn't adequately describe the report we gave. Captain Janaina's ship was most definitely a caravel, as I said a few minutes ago and as was reported yesterday. A caravel, Professor, not a pirogue." He paused and then continued. "Also, the captain herself was not an African. She was a native of the New World, a country called Quonambec."

As Beck seemed to be trying to respond to those comments, Cabot continued, "Professor, was there something else you would like me or my wife to elaborate on?"

Beck said, "Yes, there is. The racial makeup of that island where you encountered this woman Janaina—natives, Africans, Spaniards, people speaking Arabic. I find that most incredible. How in God's name could such people end up in... what's the name, Guanahani?"

Mattea spoke up during a short pause. "Professor, I can certainly understand why you would be astonished at our experience. But the short answer to your last question is that more than 50 years ago the Africans, Malians in particular, captured Spanish and Portuguese caravels off the coast of West Africa that were intent on promoting slavery in the New World. From them, including the African slaves working as crew on those ships, the Malians learned to build caravels.

In fact, ultimately, they constructed some 70 caravels and created a Malian Navy to protect the New World from European slavers."

At her response, both Professor Beck and King Henry were stunned. Then the king said, "70 caravels! That's quite a navy. And you have said the Malians have no desire to act as a military force, is that correct?"

Captain Cabot answered, "That is correct, except insofar as necessary to act in self defense. Captain Janaina explained that the peoples of the New World are simple people, peasants with no industries, no natural resources. They are farmers and fishermen. Some have learned crafts such as shipbuilding, sailing and construction of better-quality housing."

The king interjected, "And correct me if I misheard you yesterday. Did you or someone mention the Spanish Admiral Colombo? Am I mistaken?"

Mattea said, "No, you are not mistaken. There was mention of Colombo. But we did not see him when we were there. We were told that he was living in that island group, had married, and was working in some capacity for the Federation. More than that, I'm afraid we had no information."

At that point, Professor Beck had exhausted his list of concerns and simply sat back in his chair. The king sighed and arose. "Captain Cabot, Madame Jacobella, thank you for indulging the professor and myself. It has been the most interesting meeting. I look forward to seeing more of you in England. Do you have any plans beyond this?"

Mattea said, "No, Your Majesty, we have been fairly preoccupied merely with getting here. And giving our report, of course. But the captain and I have discussed the possibility of remaining here in Bristol for a time in order to sort out the many possible threads of our future. As you know, we have three sons who are quite fond of Bristol, having lived here for a time before our voyage began. Our oldest son Sebastian has become, as you know, quite an accomplished mariner. He has expressed his strong desire to continue his career under the English flag. "

The king said, "Certainly, you may stay as long as you like, and I shall look forward to helping Sebastian with his naval career."

Turning to Beck he said, "Professor, thank you for your assistance in bringing to light more information about this most interesting expedition. Please be assured that if I or the court can be of any more assistance, you have only to ask."

"Certainly, Your Majesty. I look forward to learning more about this expedition, especially the so-called New World."

With that, the king announced that he would convene a general informational meeting in about a week.

CHAPTER FOURTEEN

November 25, 1501, Bristol Harbor

Sebastian and his younger brothers were the first to see the caravels enter Bristol Harbor. It was two hours after dawn and the boys had been performing a safety check on their parents' two ships in preparation for another lesson in seamanship taught by Sebastian. "Two ships—one a Malian vessel and the other I don't recognize!" Sebastian turned to Sancio and told him to run back to the cottage and wake their parents.

It didn't take long for John and Mattea to arrive. They were astounded at the sight of the two ships, which by that time were being tied up at the dock. "John, the Malian ship—it looks like Janaina's! It is definitely a Federation ship. The Portuguese title, "Mali-Atlantico Federação", is painted on the bow. But what is the other caravel?"

"It's also a caravel, but the markings are strange, almost invisible, partially covered in blue varnish. And the people tying up both ships do not appear to be English. Some of them appear to be African, some natives of the New World."

At that point, a tall, dark, imposing woman wearing a Federation uniform walked down the gangplank of the Malian ship and along the dock to the person supervising the docking of the blue caravel. That person was a fair-skinned man wearing a rain slicker and boots. The two of them hugged, exchanged a few words, and then turned away from the ships and began walking away from the docks.

At that point they noticed that they were being watched. The woman laughed and yelled out, "Mattea Jacobella! And John Cabot! And your fine sons! Well met, my friends, well met!" Turning to her hooded companion she said, "Nicolas, say hello to my friends, the Cabot-Jacobella family!"

When Nicolas and Janaina reached the family, Janaina did the introductions. "Nicolas, this is Captain John Cabot, his wife Mattea Jacobella, and their sons Sebastian, Lewis and Sancio." She then said, "Friends, this is my very good friend and mentor, Nicolas Flamel, formerly of Paris and now from... actually, I have no idea where he now calls home."

Nicolas laughed and said, "I now call Paris home. It has always been my home, especially recently." Turning to John, he said, "Captain Cabot, I am very pleased to meet you. I suppose you're wondering why I and Captain Janaina Watu arrived here at the same time." Again, he laughed and said, "Come to think of it, I was wondering the same thing."

Cabot couldn't help but laugh as well, but he didn't know why. "It would seem you two have some plan. I wonder if it involves the meeting the king has called. Where have you come from?"

Janaina answered him, "Captain Cabot, the last time you and I met was in the island nation of Guanahani. I have to confess, Monsieur Flamel and I had a plan to join you here. And, so we have."

Mattea said, "I wish you could have arrived in time for the royal wedding of the Prince and Princess. It was held on November 14. The Prince and Princess are by now at their royal residence in Ludlow Castle in Shropshire."

Flamel said, "No, we hadn't planned on attending the wedding. But we do hope to meet with the royal family."

At that point, Father Rodrigo and Gabriel Hugo came walking up the dock from their cottage nearby. They abruptly stopped walking when they saw Flamel and Janaina talking to the Cabot family. "Well, well, well! Our old friend Nicolas cannot seem to leave us alone." Rodrigo hugged Flamel, as did Hugo, and then they greeted the others.

Janaina turned to Mattea and said, "Madame, when last we met you, the captain asked whether Admiral Colombo had survived the crossing from Spain. Well, indeed he did survive. More than survive; he and his crews now work for the Federation. When he learned of our plan to sail across the Atlantic Ocean to meet the royal family, he asked to join us. He, his wife and two children are on board as we speak. They will join us tomorrow at the king's reception in the Customs House."

* * *

The Great Admiral meets the king
November 26, 1501

The Customs House's large, open inspection area had been transformed into a grand reception room. Carpets had been laid out, and tables of different sizes and shapes had been set out around the room. On one long table, serving people had begun setting out an array of hot dishes.

The King had not arrived yet. His staff informed the guests that he should arrive in less than an hour.

Admiral Colombo's wife, Caoma, was sitting at a round table near the front of the room with Captain Janaina, Mattea, John, Sebastian, Aponi and Balder. Colombo's chair next to Caoma was empty. Caoma had the appearance of a native of the New World, with bronze-colored skin, black hair and eyes, and a slender frame. She and Janaina were talking about something amusing with Balder and Aponi. Mattea, John and Sebastian listened intently.

Seated at a square table on the left side of the room were

Sebastian's younger brothers, 17-year-old Lewis and 15-year-old Sancio, and Colombo's two daughters, Malulani and Surey. The daughters appeared to be 10 or 11 years old and strongly resembled their mother. They seemed to be enjoying talking to Lewis and Sancio.

Seated at a square table on the right side of the room were Flamel, Hassan, Father Rodrigo and Gabriel Hugo. Hassan seemed to be doing most of the talking. Flamel appeared to be distracted; he kept looking at the king's table. That table was long and rectangular and was positioned at the head of the room just inside the door. Its six chairs sat empty.

In a few minutes, a uniformed server entered the room and announced that the king would join them in a few minutes, and recommended that everyone begin eating.

After almost an hour, when the guests had just finished eating, the king came in. He was accompanied by his wife, Queen Elizabeth of York, their 6-year-old daughter Princess Mary, their 10-year-old son Prince Henry, Admiral Colombo of the Federation and Admiral Reginald Bray of the English Navy.

The king smiled and said, "Good day to my honored guests. I apologize for being late. If everyone has enjoyed their luncheon, I shall begin by explaining why I have invited you all to this gathering." He paused to allow everyone to focus their attention on the front of the room. "You all have met Admiral Colombo of the Malian-Quonambec Federation, on my left. Seated on my right is my wife, Queen Elizabeth, our son Henry Junior and our daughter Princess Mary. On their right is Admiral Reginald Bray of the Royal Navy.

"I would first like to say how much I appreciate and value the briefings I have received from everyone at this gathering, especially Captain Janaina. Admiral Bray, in particular, appreciated the information and news provided by Captain Janaina and Admiral Colombo. Perhaps it would be best if I began by asking Admiral Bray to summarize his understanding of the political situation on both sides of the Great Ocean." Turning to Bray, he said, "Admiral, at your pleasure."

The admiral stood and smiled at everyone, especially Captain Janaina. Then he spoke. "I had a most interesting discussion with Captain Janaina and Admiral Colombo. Perhaps `interesting' is too mild a word. `Astonishing' would better convey my reaction upon hearing what they had to say.

"First and foremost was learning of the existence of what those two leaders of the Federation created under the name of the "Mali-Atlantico Federação". Why was the name originally in Portuguese, you may wonder? Well, it turns out that the founders of that federation were Portuguese-speaking people from Mali and Portugal. Two of our guests today—Father Rodrigo and Monsieur Nicolas Flamel—will perhaps explain that connection at another time.

"But the most important fact, at least to me, a military man in command of a modest navy, was what was proposed at our meeting—a proposal that was most enthusiastically agreed to by our monarch and myself. Ladies and gentlemen, England as of today is now a proud associate of this Federation, which seeks to ensure the peace and prosperity of the countries on both sides of the ocean. Our two navies will go far towards meeting that goal!

"England's navy consists of some 14 ships—the Sweepstake, the Mary Fortune, the Grace à Dieu, the Governor, the Martin Garcia, the Mary of the Tower, the Trinity, the Falcon, the Bonaventure, the Caravel of Eu, the King's Bark, the Margaret, the Regent, and the Sovereign. The Federation's navy consists of over 70 ships, almost all of them fast-sailing, maneuverable caravels.

"Now, of course, England is at peace with everyone—or should I say almost everyone. The Royal Family is now well situated with respect to Spain with the marriage of our Prince Arthur and Aragon's Princess Catherine. Our relations with Portugal are excellent thanks to the work of Father Rodrigo here; our relations with the Dutch,

Germans and Italians are peaceful. We hope to expand our relations with the Queendom of Navarre.

"It is only with the French that we have had any worries. Presently we are at peace. But that hasn't always been true, as we all know. Since the turn of this century, France has been engaged in the Habsburg-Valois Wars for the takeover of several Italian city-states. We do not know if those wars will continue, or what adventures France will embark on after the Italian wars end.

"King Henry has come up with a brilliant plan to keep France from becoming our enemy once again. I am not at liberty to discuss that plan at present. In any event, it is still merely a plan. Perhaps it will come to fruition; we shall see."

Admiral Bray paused when the king signaled that it was time that the meeting be concluded. He announced, "Friends and esteemed guests, there are many important matters to be discussed later today. I sincerely hope we will have some exciting news to announce in two days time! For now, let us enjoy what's left of this glorious autumn before Old Man Winter announces his arrival!"

CHAPTER FIFTEEN

The "Malian-Atlantic Federation" is expanding

That evening, November 26, 1501, the king called for a meeting to be held in a week, on December 3, 1501, at Ludlow Castle in Shropshire, residence of Prince Arthur and Princess Catherine of Aragon. Arthur, Catherine and Catherine's mother, Queen Isabella of the two Spanish kingdoms of Castille and Aragon, were already at the Castle. Henry sent his messenger to inform Colombo, Cabot, Mattea, Janaina, Aponi, Nicolas and Hassan of the meeting.

They and the king had already had preliminary discussions about a very important topic—the creation of a royal English/Malian delegation to approach certain leaders of Europe and urge them to join the proposed "Malian-Atlantic Federation." They would discuss how best to counteract imperialistic and destructive monarchical movements wherever they threaten the peace, for example several such movements in central and eastern Europe—primarily Germany, Austria, Italy and Russia.

The first three invitees—Nicolas, Janaina and Aponi—arrived on December 3. Janaina and Aponi had earlier learned that Queen Isabella was known for putting mercury on her skin as a cure for insect bites, so they decided to warn her against the practice. "Master

Flamel is, as you perhaps have heard, an expert in alchemy and is familiar with the properties of dangerous substances. Mercury is one of the most dangerous." Isabella was surprised at this, but agreed to cease using mercury on her skin.

At that point Janaina told her that wearing one of Gabriel Hugo's rings would provide further protection against disease, she replied that she and her husband had already begun wearing their rings.

By the end of that week, on December 10, 1501, the group had decided to send representatives to Queen Anne of Brittany, Muhammad of Granada, commonly known as "Boabdil", and the parents of Anne of Navarre. The goal would be to encourage them to unite in the newly created Federation.

King Henry explained the plan to those assembled at Ludlow Castle. "Prince Arthur has managed to get my wife Queen Elizabeth of York to agree to take our younger son Prince Henry Junior to Navarre to conclude the ongoing negotiations with Anne's parents, King John of Navarre and Queen Catherine of Navarre. The negotiations concern the proposed marriage of our 10-year-old son Henry to their 10-year-old daughter Princess Anne. Arthur's mother-in-law, Queen Isabella, would accompany them in order to discuss the importance of Navarre joining the Federation. As she told me yesterday with a smile, `I'm fairly certain that those who control Navarre will be most relieved to learn that Spain no longer has any plans to absorb them!'"

"At the same time, John, Mattea, Father Rodrigo, Hugo and Janaina will travel to Brittany and meet with Queen Anne of Brittany. She currently resides in Amboise, in the Loire Valley, Brittany. Her residence is the Château du Clós Luce.

"They will urge her to join the Federation in order to counteract the power of her husband, King Louis, who ceaselessly strives to stifle Anne's efforts to maintain Brittany's independence from France. We hope that Anne will be particularly receptive to the proposal presented to her, especially when Captain Janaina describes the Federation's origin and current status.

"Here is what we propose: In order to prevent the absorption of Brittany into France, the Federation would assist Anne in keeping Louis from completing that absorption. The Federation would do this by preventing Anne's "historical" death from a kidney stone attack on January 9th,1514. In order to achieve that, the envoys would convince her to constantly wear one of the emerald-green chrome tourmaline rings crafted by Gabriel Hugo.

"I will remind you all of the information provided to us by Monsieur Flamel that in what he calls the 'alternate' future, Anne would fall ill and die of a kidney stone attack. The ring crafted by Gabriel Hugo contains one of the powerful stones obtained by Flamel's colleague, Captain Hassan of Mali. That stone is known in Quonambec and throughout the New World to have great healing powers. Queen Isabella has already received two of Hugo's rings for the same reason and she and King Ferdinand have begun wearing them.

"Anne of Brittany is a well-known advocate of preserving her country's independence. She is no longer a child, but a Dowager Queen, and determined to ensure the recognition of her rights as sovereign Duchess from that point forward. Although Louis exercises the ruler's powers in Brittany, he formally recognizes his wife's right to the title 'Duchess of Brittany' and issues decisions in her name. Anne has personally retained rights to the duchy, and the couple's second child, whether son or daughter, would be Anne's own heir, thus keeping the duchy separate from the throne of France. If the emerald-green chrome tourmaline ring she will wear prevents her untimely demise, she will remain de facto Queen of Brittany far longer than her husband Louis XII."

The king paused, took a sip of water, and then breathed deeply before continuing. "Now, moving on. Nicolas, Hassan, Colombo and Aponi—you all have a very difficult, yet interesting, task. You will travel to Granada to convince the powerful Muslim King Boabdil of the wisdom of joining the Federation. Captain Hassan is included in the delegation because of the added influence of a fellow Muslim, especially a Muslim with the powerful rank of Captain in the Malian Federation's Navy.

"Colombo's presence in that delegation will no doubt astonish and please King Boabdil, who had believed that Spain's Admiral Colombo had been lost in the Atlantic Ocean, but has now become an emissary of peace from Queen Isabella and King Ferdinand.

"Finally, the presence of Aponi, an Onondaga woman from a different region of the New World from Captain Janaina, who is from Quonambec, like Hassan. Aponi will further reinforce Boabil's confidence in the Federation's peaceful motives, since she represents those of the far north of the New World, very far from Quonambec.

"I think I have adequately set out the parameters of your tasks. The substance of your negotiations you already know—Janaina had earlier negotiated with Prince Arthur concerning the precise relationships the parties envision between Europe and the Federation. Each delegation will present those ideas to their respective recipients."

CHAPTER SIXTEEN

An eavesdropper in Navarre
January 5, 1502

Ten-year-old "Infanta Ana," as Anne d'Albret of Navarre was known to those who followed the doings of the Spanish royalty, sat in her small study listening to her Latin teacher drone on about the superiority of Latin over Spanish and all the other languages of Europe. "Except French, of course," Anne interjected. She knew the remark would annoy her teacher, but so be it. She was tired of Latin. She knew it as well as she knew French, but not nearly as well as she knew English.

When she thought of English, she decided to interject another remark that would annoy her tutor. "Even English is superior! It's certainly more useful than this dead language you're teaching me!"

Maria, her spinster teacher, tried to maintain her composure. To do so, she decided to change the subject to one she suspected would intrigue her little vixen of a student. "Ah, English. You might be interested to hear what I heard only last week. A secret, but one that I think I can trust you not to share with anyone until you learn of it from your mother and father themselves."

Anne was skeptical of secrets, especially a secret supposedly known by servants. But her curiosity won the day. "Oh, my beloved Maestra Maria. I think you should tell me! Does it concern me?"

"Concern you? It should say so. But you must promise me you will not breathe a word of it to anyone. Now, I must confess, I have not heard all the details. Only that it concerns a marriage proposal."

"A marriage proposal? Concerning whom? And why do you mention this after I praise the English language?"

"The proposal, if it comes to pass, concerns you, of course. Your future is being plotted as we speak, if you must know. And it concerns someone from England."

This piece of information hit Anne square in the chest, and she stood and walked to the window to get some air. She turned back to Maria and said, "And that's all you heard? That my parents are discussing marrying me off? Did you happen to hear who the lucky groom-to-be is?"

"I did, but I am not sure I heard correctly, or that the source of the rumor was correct. But be patient; I think you will come into possession of this information in the next few days, if my information is correct."

*   *   *

Patience is a virtue, or so they say.

More than two weeks later, just as Anne was about to brave her parents' anger and demand an answer to the rumor Maria had revealed, her mother, Catherine, came into her bedroom and told her to follow her into the kitchen.

Once there, Catherine ordered Anne to sit while she made sure they were alone. Then she closed the doors, turned back to Anne, and said, "My dear, your father and I have some good news. We have concluded our negotiations with the English and have agreed to King Henry's proposal that you become the bride of his son Henry Junior. Now, I'm sure this news will surprise you. But it shouldn't alarm you, for two reasons. First, the wedding will not take place for at least several more years. And second, the prince is, by all accounts, very handsome and very clever. And, perhaps third and best of all, the English royal family is one of the richest families in all of Europe!"

Because of what Maria had already disclosed, Anne was not as surprised as her mother might have expected. But the confirmation made her heart pound. "Mother! Why wasn't I included in those negotiations? I am very, very offended that you have so little trust or confidence, not to mention respect, that you do such a thing without my knowledge!" Anne was striving mightily to produce the required appearance of outrage, which was difficult given her underlying excitement that was actually quite a pleasant sensation.

Her mother frowned and said, "Be patient, my child. And remind yourself that as a royal daughter, you have virtually no say in such matters. Besides," she added with a half smile, "despite your best efforts, you cannot hide your delight at your prospect.

"Your father and I are working out the arrangements for you to meet Prince Henry. He may come here, or you may go there, or the two of you may meet somewhere else. We will keep you informed. Just trust us. That is all."

CHAPTER SEVENTEEN

Queen Anne of Brittany has surprise visitors in Morlaix
February 5, 1502

Queen's Butler Edwyn Galou came into the parlor where Queen Anne was having breakfast. "Your Highness, you may have visitors who wish an audience with you. An exotic ship has just dropped anchor some half a nautical mile from the Port. The messenger described it as a caravel, one of the ships popularized in the past century by the Portuguese. The messenger said the caravel had to anchor that far out because the ship's draft is about 10 feet, and our port is not that deep.

"The messenger also said the ship is brightly painted with 'Malian-Quonambec Federation' on the sails.

"Here is the description of the passengers provided by the messenger after they arrived in port on their ship's boats." The butler paused and then consulted the list. "The Malian ship's Captain is a woman named Janaina Watu. The Mates are John Cabot and his wife Mattea Jacobella, both originally from Italy but of late having returned from an exploratory voyage to the New World with a small fleet of English ships.

"The two passengers on the Malian ship are Father Martim

Rodrigo and Gabriel Hugo. The 10 members of the crew are not named." He looked up, scratched his head and continued, "According to the port messenger, Your Highness, they are the most unusual group of visitors the messenger says he has ever seen."

"How, so, Edwyn?"

"Captain Janaina Watu wears a military uniform of some type never seen before. She is a woman of unusual height and has a dark complexion. The priest might be Portuguese, judging from his name, and Monsieur Hugo is likely French. Well… they are waiting at the Welcome House at the port. They request an audience with you. They claim they are emissaries of the English king, Henry. Shall I send word for them to proceed here?"

"Thank you, Edwyn. Please send a word to have them meet me here at noon. And, also, please have my other visitors here depart for the duration of the visit."

After Edwyn left, Anne pondered this news of a proposed visit from English emissaries. She was naturally wary, of course. But also intrigued. Keenly aware of the terrible relations between France and England, Anne considered the possibility that England and Brittany might join together to keep French King Louis from his persistent attempts to subjugate Brittany to his rule. It was with this thought in mind that she prepared for the visit.

* * *

Going over the agenda

Mattea returned to the visitors' lounge at the Morlaix Port's Welcome House. "I have to say, Janaina, I am intrigued and more than a little nervous about what kind of reception we might receive from the Queen. Or should we address her as Duchess?"

"Queen," Janaina looked up from the note she had received from Anne's messenger. "As we learned from King Henry, Anne is the de facto ruler of the whole of Brittany. Her husband Louis allows her to keep her title as Queen, but insists that her true role is the largely ceremonial one of Duchess.

"As we discussed back in Bristol, we simply must gain her confidence and cooperation in our endeavor. The whole of Europe's security depends on it. These monarchies throughout virtually all of Europe are corrupt, and they pose a serious obstacle to peace throughout the greater region. Louis himself is only waiting for Anne to die so he can consolidate all power to himself. God protect us if that should come to pass."

Hugo chuckled, "Ah, but we have a present for Queen Anne that should ensure that she will not die before her time. Surely not before Louis dies." Pulling out from his pocket a small, ornately carved wooden box, he opened it to reveal the beautiful little ring sitting in its bed of silk. "The wondrous gem in this gold ring, as you know, is an emerald-green chrome tourmaline. We envision and pray that the rulers of all our allies in Europe will wear them for protection against early death from many types of illness prevalent on the continent."

John Cabot spoke after Hugo put the ring box back in his pocket. "King Henry gave me some information about the port and city of Morlaix, especially the peculiar houses there. The Queen owns one of the most spectacular homes. The homes are built in a style called `Pondalez,' meaning they are organized around a large central space which rises on at least three levels with an oak staircase decorated with a carved corner post. The galleries serving the floors are called `aisle bridges.'

"The merchants who thrive in Morlaix are linen traders specializing in a type of fine linen that is a local speciality. The timbered houses built by these merchants have a smaller ground floor surface area that grows with each added floor, creating architectural overhangs that keep the lower timbers and merchandise dry."

Cabot paused and smiled before continuing. "Apparently, these linen merchants build their houses that way in order to avoid excessive taxes, which are based on the square footage of the ground floor area."

Father Rodrigo added, "Now, in our discussions with the Queen, we must stress that our Federation is strongly committed to religious freedom. King Henry wishes to convey to Anne that although he is a devout Catholic, he wishes to ensure that other Faiths in Europe are protected. Including the Jewish faith, which our beloved Mattea professes, and the Muslim faith of Spain that our colleague Hassan professes. Our royal colleague Isabella of Spain has pledged to prevent further religious conflict instigated by the Catholic hierarchy there.

"And as our wise friend Nicolas Flamel has warned us, fewer than 20 years from now in the `alternate' future history he has visited and studied, all of Europe would be embroiled in what would be known as the `Protestant Reformation' led by a German priest by the name of Martin Luther. In order to prevent that from occurring, we will need to put pressure on the Church hierarchy to institute reforms.

"Now, of course, we shall not discuss the future with Queen Anne. Our mission is to seek her cooperation with the Federation and recognition of minority religious rights, especially Jewish and Muslim rights."

*   *   *

Meeting at the Queen's 'Pondalez'

Although the visitors had been apprised of the characteristics of the houses and buildings in Morlaix, the Pondalez-style homes took their breath away. The visitors' coach deposited them in front of the Queen's residence, they stood still in a sort of trance absorbing the exotic beauty of it before they "came to" and went to the door.

If the emissaries were impressed by the beauty of the residence, they were stunned by the beauty of the 25-year-old Queen herself. Once the royal butler, Edwyn Galou, escorted them into the parlor, they were greeted warmly by the Queen. "Welcome, visitors from England. Please, have a seat and make yourselves comfortable. I am honored by your visit. And I am hopeful that your visit portends a blossoming relationship with England.

"Now, before we begin discussing the purpose of your visit, would you be so kind as to introduce yourselves. I am told that none of you are actually English. Is that right?"

Father Rodrigo spoke first. "You are correct, Highness. Although King Henry asked us to pay you a visit, we are not English. I am from Portugal, but before that I was a missionary priest in East Africa. My friend Gabriel Hugo here is a renowned jeweler from Paris. Lady Mattea Jacobella, sitting next to Monsieur Hugo, is originally from Venice, then later from Spain, before moving to England with her husband, John Cabot, sitting here to my right."

John said, "Your Highness, I am originally from Genoa. Mattea and I lived in Spain for a few years before moving to England. We convinced King Henry to finance two expeditions across the Atlantic Ocean in hopes of reaching China."

John cleared his throat and continued, "When we made landfall on the shores of a large continent west of Iceland, we met people there who informed us that China was thousands of miles on the other side of that continent. From there we sailed to the island nation of Guanahani, which is where we met our colleague here, Captain Janaina Watu. I shall ask her to introduce herself and explain our mission here."

Anne interjected, "Wait, please. When you crossed the Atlantic Ocean, did you learn anything about the expedition of Spain's Cristoforo Colombo? I believe his fleet embarked some 8 or 9 years ago and hasn't been heard from since. It is believed that the expedition came to a bad end."

Janaina answered, "Yes, we in fact encountered Colombo, Your Highness. I am Captain Janaina Watu of the Malian-Quonambec Federation. The Federation was created jointly by people from Mali and the New World, more specifically, the peoples of Mali, Africa, and Quonambec, the southern continent directly across the Atlantic from Africa.

"Regarding the fate of Colombo, his expedition reached Guanahani. He and his entire crew joined the Federation. Many of them, including Colombo, married local people and have raised families. It is the Federation that we wish to speak to you about. Do we have your leave?"

Queen Anne nodded and said, "Please, go ahead. I'm sure I will have questions as you proceed."

"Our Federation came into being out of concerns that certain monarchies in Europe were bent on colonizing and brutalizing what is now called the New World. We, the original inhabitants of the New World, joined with Africans who had been enslaved by a fleet of Portuguese explorers. With those Africans, we created a large navy from the caravels we confiscated from the Portuguese and Spanish. We have created a bulwark against further threats from the European monarchies.

"England as of today is now a member of our Federation. Our member countries seek to ensure the peace and prosperity of the countries on both sides of the ocean. Our combined navies will go far towards meeting that goal!

"England's navy consists of some 14 ships—the Sweepstake, the Mary Fortune, the Grace à Dieu, the Governor, the Martin Garcia, the Mary of the Tower, the Trinity, the Falcon, the Bonaventure, the Caravel of Eu, the King's Bark, the Margaret, the Regent, and the Sovereign. The Federation's navy consists of over 70 ships, almost all of them fast-sailing, maneuverable caravels.

"We have been successful so far. Our Federation navy repeatedly attacked the Portuguese and Spanish ports and fleets. In our attack on Portuguese ports, we disguised our ships as ships of Spain. And in our attack on the Spanish ports, our ships were disguised as Portuguese ships. The result of our destruction of the Portuguese and

Spanish shipping has been that those two countries are now powerless to extend their reign of terror across the Atlantic Ocean. In fact, one of the monarchs of Spain, Queen Isabella, has realized the hopelessness of their military efforts and has joined in our effort to bring Europe to its senses."

Anne smiled and interjected, "Yes, I was aware of the attacks on Spanish and Portuguese shipping, but I am surprised, and somewhat delighted if truth be told, to hear of your deception! But what is Isabella's role now in your organization?"

"She has agreed to be part of our mission to recruit the support of the Kingdom of Grenada. As astounding that must seem to you, the ruler there, Boabdil, has shown some interest in meeting with our delegation. As I said, Queen Isabella is an active participant in that effort."

This piece of information caused Anne to pause for a minute. "Now, Grenada! I confess to being more than a little surprised to hear that the Spanish monarchs are no longer striving to rid Spain of Muslims." After a brief hesitation, she added, "But what about the Jews of Spain? Are they also to be left alone?"

Mattea smiled and responded. "Indeed, they are, Your Highness! I am a Jew myself, a fact that King Henry himself is aware of. Moreover, he has taken steps to rein in the antisemitism of the Church.

"Also, one of our members who will be in the delegation to Grenada is a Muslim—Hassan ibn Awolu of Quonambec. He is the son of one of the African founding members of the Federation."

Again, Anne was speechless. Then, before responding to this news, she noticed her cook standing nearby. Anne arose and said, "My dear guests, I believe it is time we took our midday meal. I see my chef standing in the entryway to the dining room. Let us resume our conversation over lunch!"

*   *   *

A lifesaving gift for the Queen

The luncheon was animated. Queen Anne was pleased at the questions regarding her husband, King Louis. "His domestic policies and programs are very popular here in Brittany. But his adventures in other lands have not gone well; in fact, they have ended in disaster. I hope he will pay more attention to matters at home. I believe he is more concerned about his health, and perhaps that concern combined with his domestic popularity will finally convince him to abandon his foreign adventures."

Her comment prompted Father Rodrigo to bring up the subject of the special ring Hugo had made for her. "Highness, you are no doubt aware of the prevalence of disease throughout Europe at the present time. Our group has learned of a very effective type of protection against these diseases. My good friend Gabriel here is a renowned jeweler in Oporto and before that in Paris. He learned of a gemstone from the New World that emanates a subtle energy capable of warding off some diseases."

Turning to Gabriel, the priest said, "My friend, why don't you bring out the ring you have crafted?"

Gabriel reached into the girdle purse he had brought into the room and pulled out a small, beautifully carved wooden box. Handing it to the Queen, he said, "Highness, we would like you to have this. We hope it will protect your health."

Anne took the box, opened it, and gasped. "This ring is beautiful!" Taking it out, she slipped it onto a finger. "It fits perfectly. The gold is beautiful, as is the stone. What is the stone?"

"It is an emerald-green chrome tourmaline from the New World. Our colleague Hassan was able to obtain several dozen of the stones from his sources in Quonambec. I have fashioned several rings with the stones, and given them to a number of royals in our membership. The native peoples of the New World wear the stones in different types of jewelry. The beneficial effects are well known."

The Queen smiled. "I thank you, Monsieur Hugo. I think I shall always wear it; I am very fond of jewelry!" She was quiet for a moment and then said, "Now, I had a question. What was it?... Oh yes, about this Federation you have created. While I have a certain amount of freedom in my domain, I must beware of giving Louis any reason to suspect my loyalties to him and France, even though I am ruler of a more or less independent country. Tell me more about this Federation. Is it primarily a military organization?"

Janaina answered, "No, Your Highness. Although we do have a substantial navy with fighting experience, our main objective is to raise the standards of living of the peoples of Quonambec, Guanahani and Mali. You see, Highness, although those peoples are primarily subsistence farmers and craftsmen, our natural resources are abundant. Our Federation hopes to promote trade and mutual assistance pacts with the nations of Europe."

Anne nodded and thought for a moment before responding. "I suspect a trade agreement might be achieved. For example, Europe has many industries that manufacture products such as clothing and metal goods. We also export farm products. What types of products are produced in the New World?"

Janaina said, "We have massive forests and mines of rare gems in Quonambec and Mali, and fisheries all around the islands of Guanahani, as well as farms that raise crops and animals. I am hopeful we can craft a trade arrangement."

At that point in the luncheon, Queen Anne was reminded by her secretary that she had another meeting in an hour. She made that announcement and the meeting came to an end.

CHAPTER EIGHTEEN

April 15, 1502; arrival in Grenada

As Nicolas's caravel approached the southern coast of Spain, he called a meeting of his fellow "conspirators," as he called them—Hassan, Colombo and Aponi. "Let me remind everyone that we will be presenting our proposal to Muhammad the Twelfth, Emir of Granada. He is 42 years old and is known as Boabdil. He is the twenty-second ruler of the Emirate of Granada. He should remember that we were coming, because Queen Isabella sent a message to him as soon as King Henry presented his plan to our group.

"Hassan, we will be counting on you to make a good impression on him as you introduce us. You might point out that many of the original founders of the Federation were Muslims from Africa.

"And you should also point out two important facts. First, the King of England has pledged to eliminate prejudice towards Jews in England. And second, one of our members in the Federation is a Jewish woman from Venezia, Italy, Mattea Jacobella.

"The reason I mention these two facts is that the only non-Muslim population of any significance within the emirate are Jews, who are generally concentrated in certain cities. Among them are long-established families who have lived here for generations as well as recent arrivals from the Christian north. Of the latter, some had fled during the Christian advance in the 13th century, fearing political change, while others fled later during persecutions under Christian rule.

"The largest community is in Granada. The Jewish population within the emirate has been estimated at around 3000. As of ten years ago, 110 Jewish households were counted in Granada. Jews are prominent in professions such as merchants, interpreters or translators, and as doctors/physicians.

"Boabdil granted Jews a protected status called `dhimmi' that gave them legal rights to their religion and a certain legal autonomy for their community. We certainly want to reinforce his decision."

Nicolas paused, then turned to Colombo and Aponi. "You will talk about the discovery of the New World. The European discovery, that is. Others discovered it thousands of years ago, crossing to the New World from the continent to its west that includes China. The New World was well populated before the Spanish fleet arrived in Guanahani. You should emphasize the inclusive nature of the Federation, pointing out that you, Colombo, are married to a native woman and have children with her.

"Aponi, you as well might speak of its diversity, as you are an Onondaga woman from a group of people who live in the far north of the New World who have developed a sophisticated civilization. You could describe your meeting with the three leaders of the Haudenosaunee Confederacy in that land, Tekahawíta, Jikonhassee and Ayenwatha."

After the meeting was concluded, the voyage continued for another half hour. Nicolas decided to drop anchor a few nautical miles west of the Port of Malaga, just inside the Strait of Gibraltar, since the sun had set. "We should plan on resuming our voyage at dawn and hope to reach the port a few hours later."

Late the next morning, the caravel dropped anchor at the Port of Malaga. Nicolas took charge of the docking and let the 8-man crew know they should stay in the Port area until permission was granted by the Port authorities for them to visit the city.

When the ship was securely tied up, Nicolas, Hassan, Colombo and Aponi began walking up the hill to the Emir's castle, which was called the "Alcazaba." It was a fairly warm day in mid-April, and the walk uphill was steep. The group was relieved when they were met by two guards at the gate of the castle, who informed them they should wait until the Emir had been informed of their arrival and permission to enter the castle was granted.

They didn't have to wait long at all. Within half an hour, a messenger arrived and escorted them into the Emir's office in the castle.

Nicolas was surprised at how ill the Emir appeared. He was known to be somewhat short, but now he looked bent and shaky. The Emir, aware of Nicolas's reaction, said, "Yes, I am not the man I used to be. I'm afraid that although my kingdom is no longer at war with the combined Castille-Aragon kingdom, the battles they waged against Granada have afflicted our people considerably, especially me."

Colombo answered, "Not only your kingdom, Your Excellency, but Spain's as well."

The Emir looked at Colombo with a puzzled expression but then replied. "Yes, I am aware of that. Queen Isabella herself told me as much when she communicated her realm's official declaration of peace. And it came none too soon, I must say! My kingdom has been severely weakened, as have I."

The Emir motioned to seats across from his desk and said, "Please, take your seats. Let us be comfortable." As everyone sat down, the Emir said, "Isabella's message also informed me of the substance of your visit. You wish to invite Grenada to join your so-called Federation, is that right?"

Flamel answered first. "That is correct. Let me first introduce the members of this delegation. I am Nicolas Flamel of Paris. To my right is Admiral Cristoforo Colombo of Spain, whose voyage to the New World did not quite reach China but was a success in other ways. Next to the Admiral is one of the inhabitants of the New World, Aponi, an Onondaga woman. And at the end is Hassan ibn Awolu, an officer in the Federation's navy."

The Emir's look of surprise was palpable. "I must say I am overwhelmed by this information. You have introduced a young woman from the New World, the Spanish admiral who was long thought to have been lost at sea, and a Muslim man of African appearance! I must acknowledge the young lady first. Aponi, I am honored to meet someone from the New World." Turning to Colombo, he said, "Admiral, I am honored by your visit and look forward to learning more about your voyage." Then, to Flamel, he said, "Monsieur Flamel, I have heard so much about you. Welcome to my kingdom." And then the Emir turned to Hassan and said, "Salaam alaikum, Hassan! I did not expect to see a fellow Muslim in your delegation. Welcome to Granada!"

The Emir seemed a bit breathless, but then recovered and asked Aponi to say something about herself.

"Your Eminence, my people are from a distant land across the western sea. They are the Onondaga people. I was but a girl on one of their boats when a group of our enemies, the Mikmak people, attacked us as we were exploring the strait to the southwest of an island known as Beothuk. I alone was rescued, saved by people from the island and adopted by an elder there named Dogajavik."

The Emir was silent for a moment. Then he nodded and said, "I would like to hear more, but first, Admiral Colombo, tell me about your voyage. Why did you not return to Spain to report on your success?"

Colombo smiled, "Well, Your Eminence, we encountered a great civilization where we landed. The people there welcomed our crew and invited us to join them. That was when we learned of the Federation, which my colleague Hassan will describe."

The Emir turned to Hassan and said, "Tell me about yourself first, please."

Hassan cleared his throat and said, "Your Eminence, mine is a very humble story, although my forebears' stories are noble.

"My full name is Hassan Ali. I am a grandson of Sofia Amina and Hassan Jibril, who had named their son Awolu ibn Jibril in honor of Awolu, one of the African slaves who had been rescued from the docks at Lagos, Portugal when the Malians burned those docks and captured several caravels in 1459. Sofia and Hassan's son Awolu then married and had a son, me, Hassan Ali."

The Emir said, "Ah, so the story I have heard of Malian ships attacking Spain disguised as Portuguese ships is true! Fascinating! I certainly want to hear more about this Malian navy, or is it the so-called Federation navy?"

"The navy is the Federation's. The Federation is an economic and self-defense association composed of Quonambec, Guanahani, Mali and other nations on both sides of the Great Ocean. England, France, Navarre, Brittany and most of Spain are the latest members. We invite Your Eminence to join us on behalf of Al Andaluz and the rest of Spain."

The Emir sat back in his chair and took a deep breath. "You say economic and self-defense. I assume by economic you mean trade and exploration. But tell me more about self-defense. From what or whom?"

"From the decaying monarchies, primarily, Your Eminence. All over Europe royal families are increasingly self-destructive and dangerous to one another. You only have to ponder the history in Spain itself to begin to understand how much more dangerous the situation is becoming in the rest of Europe."

"But what kind of aid can the Kingdom of Grenada provide? We have no coastline on the Great Ocean, only the Mediterranean."

Hassan nodded and said, "You can do much with our aid. The Italian states are in a perennial state of war with each other and with other countries. They send armies to the Holy Land and attack the peoples there, Muslims and Jews... and even Christians whom the Italians believe to be Muslims because of the way they dress and because they speak Arabic."

"Yes, I have heard of those organized forays into the Holy Land. Most are instigated by the Church, is what I have heard. They are called `Crusades.'"

"Certainly, the Church is part of the reason, but the wealthy in Europe also provide material aid to those crusades."

"You say my kingdom can help. How so? We have no navy, and our army was decimated by the Catholic monarchs during their war with us."

"Your Eminence, the Federation possesses a navy of over 70 ships, and as you have noted, our navy has engaged in battles in the past. We can do so again. With your leave, the Federation could deploy a few ships to your port at Malaga. Those ships would remain under the joint command of the Federation and your kingdom. That Malagan navy could do much to interrupt the attacks of the Italians on the innocent people of the Holy Land."

Hassan's explanation seemed to perk up the Emir. At least for a moment. But then he slumped back in his chair and sighed. "But I fear I have no energy left after the long-running disputes with the Catholics."

Nicolas smiled and said, "Your Eminence, perhaps we have a remedy for your lack of energy." Reaching into his bag, Nicolas pulled out a small wooden jewelry box and handed it to the Emir. "Open it, Your Eminence."

The Emir did so and gasped. "Oh, my. A ring. A golden ring with an exotic gem of a type I have never seen! What is it?"

"The stone is an emerald-green chrome tourmaline. My colleague Hassan is from Quonambec, across the Great Ocean. He found a source of these stones and obtained several dozen. Another colleague of ours, Gabriel Hugo, a master jeweler from Paris, fashioned gold rings with these stones. So far, our Federation has presented rings to rulers throughout western Europe."

The Emir slipped the ring onto his finger and exclaimed, "It fits beautifully. But you say it has some sort of healing energy. How so?"

"The natives of Quonambec wear jewelry made from these stones as a way of warding off disease. From what we hear, the stones are indeed very effective. I urge you to wear this ring; perhaps it will restore your energy for your tasks ahead."

*   *   *

The Emir invited the guests to a luncheon. Other notables in his kingdom attended as well. When the Emir announced the idea of joining the Federation, the notables were unanimous in their approval. Hassan congratulated them and said to the Emir, "Eminence, I propose to send four or five of our caravels to your harbor to act as a fledgling navy for Granada. You may appoint a commander and other officers as you deem appropriate. I would also recommend you employ shipbuilders to begin building other caravels."

"That would be wonderful. I accept your offer!"

At that point, the luncheon came to an end and the other guests started leaving. Nicolas asked the Emir if he had heard of the famous scholar and mystic Abraham Zacuto. The Emir looked shocked. "How do you know about Dayyan Abraham?"

Nicolas smiled and said, "I have studied his work for many years, Your Eminence. I finally met him some 20 years ago in Salamanca." Nicolas glanced around the room to make sure everyone else had left and then continued. "Your Eminence, I was trained in Paris as an alchemist. When I heard of an eminent scholar of oceanic navigation in Spain, I traveled there to meet the man who perfected a navigation device called the astrolabe. I wanted to tell him of my modifications of the device, but he was too concerned about the persecutions against Jews in Spain to really sit down and have a discussion with me. I believe he was planning to move to Portugal."

The Emir smiled. "That is a wonderful story, Nicolas. You will be pleased to learn that not only did the brilliant scholar not flee to Portugal, but he moved here, to my kingdom. He is my guest and gives an occasional lecture at the university. He is very old, though, and I worry about his health. He often talks about moving to the Holy Land so he can be buried in Jerusalem."

Nicolas looked surprised. "Living here, Eminence? That is the best news I have heard lately! I wonder if I might have an audience with him. I have much to tell him and I am sure he has much to say to me."

*   *   *

Meeting with Abraham Zacuto

The Emir escorted Nicolas into Zacuto's office at the rear of the castle and left them alone so they could have some privacy. Zacuto arose from his desk with some difficulty and peered at Nicolas. "Ah, I think I remember you, Monsieur Flamel. I recall you paid me a visit and wanted to discuss the astrolabe. Am I correct?"

"You are correct. That was what I wanted to talk to you about. I still would like to discuss my modifications to the astrolabe, if you would like to hear about them."

Zacuto nodded absent mindedly, but then said, "Nicolas, I'm not sure I'd have much to contribute, or even that my questions would be intelligent. I'm quite aged, of course, and my mind is not quite what it was."

Nicolas said, "Well, I have a gift for you that might help improve your health and your mind. Have you heard of the rare stone called the emerald-green chrome tourmaline?"

Zacuto nodded. "Yes, one of my colleagues years ago, a visiting scholar from Palestine, told me that indigenous peoples believe the stone has some sort of healing power. I don't recall the details, though. As I said, my mind seems to be slipping away little by little."

Nicolas handed Zacuto a small gold ring with the stone mounted on it. "Here, try this on. If it fits, you may keep it. You should always wear it. I believe you will gain some benefit from it."

Zacuto was pleased when he saw that the ring fit his finger perfectly. "I am honored, Nicolas. Let us hope the ring will do me some good. Now, what were we talking about just now? Something about what you have been doing? Was it about the astrolabe?"

Nicolas could see that a detailed discussion of the modifications to the astrolabe would not be beneficial. But he charged ahead in the hope that Zacuto would be an attentive audience, a participant even. "Abraham, many years ago, I managed to modify my own spherical astrolabe in such a way that it became not only a device for navigating the oceans, but also for navigating through time. I used it to travel to the distant future and the distant past. I learned much and have used that knowledge in helping in the discovery of the New World and, more importantly, the protection of the New World from the likes of Spain and Portugal."

It seemed that Zacuto was trying to follow Flamel's narrative, but was having some difficulty. "Travel through time, you say?… Yes, I think that might be possible with the right modifications to the device. Rare metals and gems, that sort of thing." He paused and added, "Is that what you did? You made it work?" He paused for a moment, then his eyes lit up. He laughed and said, "You found the manuscript? The one written by my professor, Isaac Aboab of Salamanca?" Zacuto was getting more excited.

Nicolas was astounded. "Yes, Professor Aboab! He's the one who discovered the way those rare metals interacted when assembled in a certain fashion. His manuscript was published in Hebrew, and I obtained a French copy in 1410. From it I was able to perfect my spherical astrolabe—I made a time machine, Abraham! A machine capable of transporting a person throughout time, the future as well as the past. And I have done it, Abraham. I have done it."

This outburst seemed to have startled Zacuto. He then seemed to slump down in his chair. "Please, Nicolas, I need to think about what you have said. Give me a moment."

Nicolas could see that Zacuto was not going to be able to keep up with the conversation, so he said, "Abraham, you have been a wonderful host, and I thank God that I was able to have this visit with you. Please, please, wear that ring always. It will help you, believe me when I say it will help you."

Zacuto smiled and said, "Thank you, Nicolas. I shall. And thank you for coming by."

When Nicolas returned to the main sitting room, he saw that the Emir was having a lively conversation with Colombo, Hassan and Aponi. "Ah, Nicolas. I hope your visit was fruitful. We have been having a wonderful time, sharing stories and making plans to meet again."

"That's wonderful, Eminence. Yes, my visit was fruitful, although I can see that Professor Zacuto tires easily. He speaks of going home to Palestine. Actually, I think such a trip might be helpful."

The guests bade farewell to their host and the group departed.

*   *   *

August 15, 1502

It was like a family reunion at King Henry's Bristol residence. All the "ambassadors" as Henry called them had returned from their mission of recruitment. Janaina, Hugo, Rodrigo, Mattea and John reported on their successful visit to Queen Anne of Brittany. King Henry's wife, Queen Elizabeth of York, returned from Navarre and reported on her successful agreement regarding the planned marriage of Prince Henry and Princess Anne. Finally, Hassan, Flamel, Aponi and Colombo reported on their successful visit with Boabdil of Malaga.

King Henry was very pleased at the successful outcome of their efforts. "Now we only have to keep a wary eye on the Ottomans and the Italians."

Nicolas said, "Well, I don't think we need to worry much longer. The Federation donated a small fleet of armed caravels to Boabdil so he could expand his navy and begin regular patrols of the Mediterranean. We can expect that the Ottomans and the Venetians will exhaust each other with their continual maritime attacks. Perhaps they will do our job for us. In any event, we envision sending envoys soon to Constantinople and Venezia to propose an agreement between them and the Federation."

Henry leaned back and smiled. "Yes, that would be wonderful indeed!" Then he paused and looked out the window before continuing. "I do hope everyone here would consider this to be an ongoing project. What I mean is that it seems to me to be something requiring regular oversight."

Janaina nodded. "Yes, Highness. For myself and the others in the Federation, that is our expectation."

Mattea and John said they anticipated remaining in England so that they could give their younger sons some sort of "normal" life. They expected Sebastian to stay with the Federation.

Aponi said she and Balder would also stay with the Federation.

Father Rodrigo and Hugo said they would return to Oporto and keep an eye on the royals there.

The king looked at Flamel. "And what about you, Nicolas? What are your plans? Back to Paris?"

"Yes, Highness, I think I need to return to Paris at some point. My home is in need of some work, and my body and mind are in need of some rest. But for now I think I shall stay in England and do some writing before retiring to my cabin here on the grounds. And after Paris… who knows? I suspect I shall pay a visit to my friends in Niumi. We shall see.

"But before I leave Paris, I have something I need Father Rodrigo to do for me." Turning to the priest he said, "Father, do you recall me telling you when you and Gabriel were at my home in Paris that I had a special task for you?"

Rodrigo thought for a moment, then said, "Yes, something to do with your spherical astrolabe?"

"That's correct. I have it here with me here in Bristol. I am tired of carrying it with me everywhere, a useless piece of baggage is what it has become. After all, it was Horacio Fuente's astrolabe that you and Gabriel modified, not mine. I would like for you to take mine home with you to the Church in Oporto. Please ask the Bishop to accept the astrolabe as a donation to the Church's archives. I feel my astrolabe will be safe there for the time being."

The priest said, "It will be my pleasure. Remind me to put it in my luggage when it is time for me to depart."

Nicolas was relieved. He knew from his travels to the future that at the end of the 19th century the Church in Oporto would empty out its archives and put everything up for auction. The Church's records of the auction listed Flamel's astrolabe as having been purchased by a Chinese diplomat named Yi Kang. Flamel read a little about him and learned that he had a reputation as a deeply superstitious man.

In one of Flamel's voyages to the future, he located Yi Kang's memoir from the 1960's. Yi Kang wrote that in 1884 while posted in the Abyssinian city of Harar, he attended an auction and purchased a 400-year-old book bound in black leather. It had Arabic and Amharic characters on the cover, neither of which Yi Kang could read. The text of the book was written in English, another language Yi Kang could not read. Flamel realized that the book had been written by Horacio Fuente and stored in a Mosque archive in Zeila, Somalia, by his daughter. It was then stolen by the deeply superstitious warlord

Ahmad Grañ, who kept it with him in all his battles. Upon Grañ's death, the book ended up in a library in Harar and was subsequently purchased by Yi Kang.

In his memoir, Yi Kang frequently stated his belief that the astrolabe and book acted together as some sort of talisman. He wrote that to protect himself he kept them with him always. In 1924, twenty years after his retirement, he bought a very old mansion in Hawaii and lived there for 40 years. In his memoir he mentioned storing the astrolabe and book in the attic.

Flamel thought of a brilliant plan. He would travel to Niumi and retrieve Khadijah's astrolabe, the one that Horacio Fuente had modified to become a time machine. Flamel would leave his own book, entitled "Um Tempo Longe do Tempo," in Khadijah's apartment, but use the astrolabe to transport him to Hawaii in 1964. He would retrieve his own astrolabe from Yi Kang's mansion and replace it with Khadijah's astrolabe.

With that firmly in his mind, Nicolas knew he could take a well-deserved rest in Paris before embarking on his trip to Niumi in a few years.

CHAPTER NINETEEN

March 21, 1506

Aliyah, a young woman on holiday from Quonambec, had come to visit her elderly great aunt Khadijah at her home in Niumi. To her surprise and sadness, Khadijah's friend Nicolas Flamel informed her that Khadijah had passed away two nights ago in her sleep. Flamel handed Aliyah a book handwritten in Portuguese and said, "Your great aunt, with my collaboration, wrote it in a language most people don't understand these days. Your dear Khadijah wanted you to keep it safe and in the family. She intended to give it to you last year, but you were unable to pay her a visit then."

She held the book in her hands and paged through it, marveling at the beautiful handwriting and binding. It was bound in black leather with chain stitching. Embossed on the leather cover was the title. "Um Tempo Longe do Tempo."

But she was puzzled at why Khadijah would write the book in Portuguese. In Aliyah's youth, she had studied Portuguese at the insistence of her great aunts Khadijah and Sofia, and her grandmother Maryam. She recalled an occasion when she was dining with her grandparents and great aunts. They were explaining why she should study Portuguese. She had complained, "But why Portuguese?

That little country in Europe is a poverty-stricken backwater, nobody goes there." She turned to her grandfather, Hassan. "You agree with me, don't you?"

"Actually, I agree with my beautiful and headstrong wife. Although I was forced to learn the language of the hated Portuguese during the year when I was a slave on a Portuguese sailing ship, I soon came to value the language. Now, of course, very few people speak it. But there is a vast literature written in Portuguese, including historical accounts of the days when Portugal dreamt of creating its plan of world domination. That plan, thanks be to God, never came to pass." Hassan paused and smiled. "The plan failed because of the wars between Portugal and Spain. The two would-be rivals for world domination through slavery and colonization repeatedly attacked one another's ships." When he said that, he chuckled and said something that Aliyah found puzzling. "Ah, I remember those battles well. Such a strategy your grandmother and her sisters devised!"

Sofia frowned at Hassan. "Dear Hassan. We mustn't spoil the surprise. Let Aliyah learn the truth of those battles when she reads the book." Then she said to Aliyah, "Please, even if you never have to use the language it's important that you know our history." Then she smiled and said, "You will learn the origin of those wars!" After she said that, she chuckled and repeated, "I think you will find Khadijah's book extremely entertaining and enlightening."

Now, years later, after not only Khadijah's passing but Sofia's and Maryam's as well, Aliyah had some free time on her hands. The last of "The Three Sisters," as they liked to refer to themselves, had passed away. So... she opened the book and began reading.

*   *   *

Nicolas Flamel makes one last trip

As Aliyah was engrossed in the book, Nicolas went into Khadijah's bedroom and retrieved the astrolabe that she and her sisters had modified, the one Father Rodrigo had inherited from Horacio Fuente. He carefully wrapped the astrolabe in a towel and placed it inside his suitcase. Then he walked out into the living room and took leave of Aliyah. "I must leave now. I hope you enjoy the book. Remember what it is—the history of how all this came to be!"

Aliyah found the comment puzzling, but hoped it would soon become clearer the more she read.

*　　　*　　　*

Flamel walked out the door, turned left and went around to the rear of the building. Looking around to make sure he was alone, he took out the astrolabe, unwrapped it, and set it on the garden ledge. He adjusted the first of the two arrows for the geographic coordinates of "Molokai, Hawaii," and the second for the date of "1964." Then he put one hand on the location arrow and his second hand on the date arrow.

As soon as he did that, the scene in front of him blurred, wavered and changed from an African garden to an asphalt road in Hawaii. He hurriedly rewrapped the astrolabe and put it back in his suitcase. He took a look around and began walking down the road towards what looked like a village in the distance.

Nicolas passed a sign that read "Kalaupapa." As he drew closer to the outskirts of the village, he saw that the area looked like it was once a grove of palm trees but was now in the beginning stages of a housing development. Several houses were under construction, but there was one magnificent 19th century mansion set back from the road on a cliff overlooking the Pacific Ocean. "That must be the one," Nicolas mumbled.

There was a "For Sale" sign posted in front of the mansion. The front door was open, and Nicolas saw two people leaving. A woman stood just inside the door and smiled as the couple left. Nicolas approached, smiled, and said, "Hello. I'm relieved to find you still here. You are the real estate agent?"

"Yes. Maryanne Clarke. And you are?"

He shook her hand and said, "Nicolas Flamel. I read the advertisement and thought I'd take a look. My taxi dropped me off at the earlier village by mistake and I've had quite a walk getting here." He paused, set down his bag and said, "Do you mind if I just walk around inside?"

"Sure. I hope you don't mind but some workmen have opened up one of the attics to inspect for roof leaks and that sort of thing. The house hasn't been occupied for a few years and you never know what kind of condition the roof and attics are in. Feel free to take a look in the attic yourself if you like. The ladder is still in place. I'll be in my car finishing up some paperwork if you have any questions."

"Thanks. Don't mind if I do. The house I previously owned had a terrible roof leak and mold in the attic, so I definitely don't want to go through that again."

Nicolas walked into the parlor, strolled around a bit, then inspected the kitchen before heading back to one of the drawing rooms. There was a ladder set up under the attic trapdoor. He looked back and didn't see the agent, so he climbed the ladder and entered the attic through the trapdoor. As he expected, it was full of junk, including a large crate in the center of the attic. Hoping it was the very same crate left in the attic by the original owner of the mansion, Yi Kang, Flamel crawled over and opened it. Inside was a steamer trunk full of old clothes. Excitedly, Flamel pulled out the clothes and there it was–"My astrolabe! My beloved astrolabe! After all these years, you are still here." He took out the astrolabe and set it aside.

Flamel opened his bag and unwrapped Khadijah's astrolabe, the one that originally belonged to Horacio Fuente. He picked up the astrolabe and firmly slammed it against one of the wooden columns holding up the roof. "I hope that breaks the silver wire the way Horacio broke it when he fell all those years ago." He lifted the astrolabe up and shook it gently. Hearing a slight rattle inside the little gold globe in the center of the astrolabe, he said, "Yes! The wire is broken! Now it will be up to João da Gama to fix it in the future." He carefully put it in the trunk of old clothes and placed the trunk back in the crate. He wrapped his own astrolabe in the towel and placed it in his suitcase. Then he crawled back to the trapdoor and climbed down the ladder.

He walked back outside to the agent's car and said, "Thanks, but this place is a bit too much for me. Not my style, either." He smiled, turned and began walking back up the road to the village. He knew the mansion would change hands several times before eventually being bought by João da Gama in 2017. None of the subsequent owners would ever bother to open, let alone inspect, the attics.

As he walked up the road he asked himself What now, Monsieur Flamel? Is my work done? He decided to take a room in the village and stay for a few days to sort his future out. Does my future involve aging? Death? Or shall I stay forever young? As he walked up to the porch of a rustic inn in the village, he reached into his shirt and caressed his amulet. Not just yet. Not just yet.

ABOUT THE AUTHOR

After 23 years practicing law with the California Attorney General's Office in San Francisco, and teaching for 13 semesters in Golden Gate's Appellate Advocacy program part time as an adjunct professor, I retired in 2011 and began writing fiction and memoirs. My first opus was a novella, *My Brother's Keeper*, loosely based on the circumstances of my younger brother's murder. Next came a novel, *Stolen Identity*, published in 2015, and its sequel, *Unfinished Business*, in 2017. *Trial and Error*, the third novel in the trilogy that began with *Stolen Identity* came out in 2021. My novel *The Mystic and the Warrior* came out in 2021.

The Starlight Commune is a combination of two previously self-published novels, *The Spherical Astrolabe* and *Around the Horn and Back*.

My short story *One More Race Before We Die* was published in 2019 in the University of Hawaii eZine, Vice-Versa. I included that story in my *Collected Stories* in 2021.

I published three memoirs in 2021: *A Pirate Forever, Life as a Peace Corps Volunteer, Ethiopia and Eritrea, 1972-74*, and *The Happy Wanderer*. While still a law student at Golden Gate, I served on the Law Review and published an article, *"Qualified Immunity for INS Church-Busters? Presbyterian Church (U.S.A.) v. United States*, Golden Gate University Law Review, Ninth Circuit Survey, Volume 20, Number 1, Spring 1990. In the year 2000 I published a memoir of my Peace Corps experience in Asmara, Eritrea, in the Peace Corps Writers anthology, *Eritrea Remembered: Recollections and Photos by Peace Corps Volunteers*.

SELECTED WORK by
MICHAEL BANISTER
(in chronological order)

My Brother's Keeper

A drug courier crashes his plane in a frozen lake in Yosemite's high country. Winston, a Yosemite "valley rat" on the run from killers in his home town, discovers the plane during a winter hike. He off loads the cargo and begins a new life as a drug dealer. After he and his girlfriend are murdered during a drug deal gone south, their two unrelated children, Josh and Kathy, are raised by their respective grandparents. When Josh asks his Uncle Mark for help in finding his "sister," the outcome is anything but predictable.

Stolen Identity

Dushan's dreams had always been unusual—sometimes scary, sometimes exhilarating. But ever since he was seven years old his dreams took on another dimension—it was like he was awake inside them. His mother—who he thought had been killed in the Yugoslavian civil war when he was a baby—was talking to him, telling him she was alive and living with his father—who was supposed to have been lost at sea during a fishing expedition in the North Sea. In each of those dreams, Dushan was unable to respond and tell his parents that he was living with his "adopted" family in California and was best friends with his "stepbrother" Danilo. The two stepbrothers were now teenagers and occasionally popped up in one another's dreams, sharing their impressions after waking up.

However, the time for dreaming was past—they were about to embark on a desperate attempt to escape their abusive father, the man who arranged to steal Dushan from his real father and plant the lie that his real parents were dead. Their attempt succeeded on one level, but the consequences were completely unexpected.

Unfinished Business

The exciting sequel to "Stolen Identity," the story of a stolen boy and his beloved "stepbrother" growing into manhood and bringing their two families together. Now, they discover they have some unfinished business to take care of and some very unpleasant people to deal with. This gripping tale follows these young men and their families through Britain, Ireland and Slovenia as they attempt to put an end to the tragedies that brought them all together in the first place.

Trial and Error

Dushan Sava was in trouble. Accused of stealing the identity of the victim of a horrific traffic accident, and then impersonating him as a college student, Dushan, an illegal immigrant, had to flee the country using the victim's passport. A year later, after having obtained his own passport and returned to the US, he accompanied a friend who would soon join the faculty at Rutgers University. Dushan's former roommate saw him on campus, and Dushan was arrested and put on trial. The outcome of the trial was anything but certain.

The Mystic and the Warrior

Who was the man who called himself Shamsuddin? In post-war Valletta, on the island of Malta, he lived in a part of the city that still hadn't recovered from the destruction of World War Two. In 1955, Shamsuddin lived in a bombed-out post office and sold antiques and other valuable items. When a group of five young men from Istanbul paid a visit looking for such things they had heard Shamsuddin could sell them, the parting gifts he provided them were much more than gifts—the young men soon discovered they couldn't bear to be without them.

Forty years later, Shamsuddin's business had radically changed. He had allied himself with Turgut Evren, a Colonel in the Turkish military. Each man had a hidden agenda—hidden from society and hidden from each other. And the five men who were no longer young? What was their destiny in this evolving story?

Life as a Peace Corps Volunteer Ethiopia and Eritrea, 1972-74

A collection of aerogrammes, memoirs and photos from my two years as a Peace Corps Volunteer in Ethiopia and Eritrea, 1972-74.

A Pirate Forever!

A memoir of my life growing up in Japan, Austria, Germany and California.

The Happy Wanderer

A collection of memoirs of my travel and work, 1974-2021, in Seattle, Tunisia, Berkeley, Turkey, Oakland and Ireland.

Collected Stories

Four stories:

One More Race Before We Die—Three race car drivers killed in a race ask a Las Vegas magician to stage a race to allow the dead drivers to finish the race.

Gino di Lampedusa—A genie on the lam from an evil genie in his own world passes through the veil and asks a Las Vegas magician to help him capture and neutralize the evil genie.

Whitethorn, 1969—a backwoods commune terrorizes a group of back-to-the-land hippies.

My Brother's Keeper—a loosely based story based on the murder of the author's drug-dealing brother.